FOREVER WITH YOU

A SWEETGUM MEADOWS ROMANCE
BOOK SIX

IMANI PRICE

First Edition: December 2023

ISBN 978-1-960207-58-6 (ebook)
ISBN 978-1-962071-98-7 (paperback)

Published by Books to Hook Publishing, LLC.
www.BooksToHook.com

CONTENTS

CHAPTER ONE

Rain brought a light drizzle creeping into the house through the open kitchen windows. India shivered as the drops hit her skin, chilling her despite the warmth of the night.

India guessed it was fitting, considering her mood.

"It's refreshing if you enjoy getting caught in it," Kim slammed shut the over-sink window. India was to her left, wiping drops of water to keep them off of the countertops. With every squeak of the surface, she added more force. Earlier, these drizzles had been sheets of showers, interrupting their movie. At first, they'd welcomed the harsh weather until India recalled her open windows. Fast forward five minutes and here they were.

The rain, like everything lately, felt both unexpected and unwanted.

India wiped imaginary sweat from her forehead. She spread her towel against the counter. "I know. If only we'd met outside under a tree. Can you imagine being soaked for our last night together?" she involuntarily pushed her bottom lip forward. Her heart ached as she watched Kim wash her hands at the sink.

"India," Kim started, a guilty smile threatening to emerge. She dried her hands on another towel hanging from a rack on the cupboards. "This isn't our last night together. It will just be our last for a while," she put the fuzzy fabric back in its place. "Now, what did I say about focusing on the negative?" She reached out and gently patted India on the shoulders.

India knew that she was pouting and being petty, but she couldn't help it. Her best friend had just returned, and she was already going to leave again.

Leaving India alone.

Yet again.

Kim had been gone for two months. She'd just returned to Sweetgum, their little town tucked in the South, last week after sightseeing for their travel content in Wyoming. She and Malik ran a tight schedule that India learned by heart so that she could keep in contact with her dear friend. What used to be Saturday afternoon strolls and weekend sleepovers morphed into video calls between her and Kim. She'd adapted to Kim's setup fairly quickly, but still longed to see her friend in the flesh. Last week and now were a blessing in what felt like years apart, but great things never lasted.

"You said not to, but it's hard," India stroked her head of braids absently. "When you and Malik start your nature show, it'll be a year before I see you again."

Kim didn't respond, her sigh tempered but still evident. India looked out on the remains of their muted girls' night. They'd paused the movie in the living room to address the rain that had sloshed into the house. From here, India saw their empty snack packets littering her table. It was a familiar scene, one that they had created many times in the past. To settle on the couch with her best friend with no fears or worries was a blessing she'd taken for granted at the time.

Now, even with Kim here, the inevitable parting plagued her mind. Sure, they shared many laughs on her couch like old times, but at the back of India's mind, sadness lurked, followed by a deep dread for what would come. She'd mostly gotten used to Kim's absence but preferred her here. For so long, Kim had been around. But with age came change; something inevitable.

India hated it.

Kim pursed her lips. "True, but we'll call and text like last time. It's not the end of the world, India," she said kindly.

India knew that. She was a rational person who understood that her friend would do the best she could to keep in touch.

And, she felt like a jerk for being so petty about all of this. Kim had every right to be doing all of the nature stuff. While on a particularly lengthy escapade in California filming for their YouTube channel, Malik and Kim were discovered by producers. Who had originally seemed like four average hikers at Redwood National Park wound up approaching them with a once-in-a-lifetime offer. Initially, Malik had rejected the deal for fear of perception, but through Kim's persuasion, he agreed. He'd found pleasure in the concept of spreading knowledge on nature. Kim wouldn't have forced him if he was adamant, but boy had she rejoiced when Malik complied.

India still remembered the joy and the excitement she had felt when Kim broke the news. If anyone deserved a show, it was them. Their YouTube series was a hit, and their relationship wholesome. Just like the videos on Kim and Malik's channel, this reality series would see them on the move. They wouldn't just be featured in national parks in America but across the globe. Her friend really had hit it big time, and India's prayers were dedicated to their success.

She didn't want for Kim and Malik to miss out on a second of that dream. It just sucked that Kim's success and the realization of her dreams meant that India would be here. Still.

Without her friend to support her. Waiting on Kim's return.

"I know," sighed India. She untangled her hands from Kim's. "You guys will kill it out there," she said sincerely.

India meant it. She would hype her best friend every single hour of every single day, even if it killed her.

Kim giggled. "Thanks. And you'll be just fine here on your own. Just like you have been during my recent trips," she tugged India to the living room where they sat once more. Neither woman had changed into sleepwear. Kim planned on sleeping over but had been hooked on movies since arriving. Both wore what they'd put on this morning. The day had been one from their dreams. They spent the Saturday meandering Sweetgum, peeking into shops, and then the movie night was a culmination of all their favorite activities. Kim's flight would take off bright and early on Sunday.

India didn't want to waste it being sad or pouting. She could do that all by herself when Kim was gone.

She heaved a breath. "Well, shall we finish the movie?"

Kim's smile brightened. "I'd say so. Those two aren't going to fall in love without us watching, you know?"

India laughed. "Yep. Let's get to it."

They settled in to watch the movie. India had one eye on the show, and one eye on her friend. She and Kim went way back, and the ritual of watching movies like this was as familiar to her as breathing.

She didn't want to waste a single second of it, not when she would miss her friend so badly when she left.

After finishing the sappy romcom they'd chosen, Kim and India sat face to face. They munched on chocolate bars purchased at the market. The bars were just one of many snacks that they had bought in honor of tonight. It was a lot of treats, sure, but they were more than just that. They were a celebration of their friendship.

And, India thought, not at all a goodbye.

"So, you're not at all nervous?" India licked her sweet lips. She peeled the wrapper like a banana and bit into the delicious chocolate. "Your videos have gotten over a million views in the past, but this is national TV. No scratch that, global TV," on top of her sadness was pure glee. Her best friend's life was taking a positive turn. Kim had found love and now prosperity. India could cry from delight.

"I wasn't nervous before, but you just might make me," Kim crossed her legs on the sofa. Her sandals were nowhere to be seen. Both she and India were barefoot. "Actually no. I'm not nervous because, like you said, we've had really successful videos before, so this is just like that. There's a chance more people will watch, but the same goes for our channel," she bit her half-eaten candy bar. "I'm more excited than anything. Even if no one watches, it's incredible to think we got scouted."

India had to agree. "Make sure you convince them to let you do more hair. I loved that segment in your videos. Keep giving hairdos to celebrities," their bodies shook as they both laughed heartily. India wiped her eyes of the soft tears that had gathered there. "Wow. I can't believe this is happening."

Kim shook her head, shifting her faux-locs. She'd done both her and India's hair. India always liked compensating Kim for her services, but this time, the woman straight-up refused to let her pay. No ifs, no buts. "It is. And it's hard for both of us but also exhilarating. Now come on," she took India's free hand. "Tell me your plans. You'll have a lot of free weekends without me. I'm not sure how much I liked what you did the last time I traveled with Malik."

"Was flipping through our high school pictures so bad?" India asked defensively. She knew the answer, because it was kind of bad, but asked anyway. "It's not like I did that all weekend," she clarified.

Both women looked up as more rain showered onto the building. They heard whistling winds outside. Something of a storm was in effect. Nothing major, but enough that they took note. The weather forecast called it heavy rain, which wasn't uncommon in this corner of Georgia. India made a note to ensure that Kim didn't drive home in worsening conditions, but other than that, the rain felt right.

It fit the mood that India was in, for sure.

She turned back to her friend. "I also went on walks alone and stopped by the park by myself too," she laid on the 'lonely best friend' act thick. "I gently tugged my cardigan around my shoulders as I wistfully looked out on the people there. I remember seeing so many friends walking side by side. Laughing, talking. Reminded me of back when I had a friend who lived in Sweetgum," she sighed, looking melodramatically into the distance. "Perhaps I could even write her a letter sometime, should the post be running this time of year."

Kim started chuckling behind her palm. "Did you send it by pony or by a passenger pigeon?"

"Neither," India pressed a hand dramatically against her forehead. "I simply tied it to a bottle and hoped it would find its way to you."

"Girl. You are too much. Extra," Kim muttered, shaking her head.

India sighed, her sad attempts at humor finally dissolving. "Are you sure you and Malik can't adopt me?"

"No, babe. We can't adopt a grown woman."

It was such a long time. Two to three months apart was okay, but a year seemed like much. India gave her friend a half-smile. "I know you guys will come back and stay to start Malik's business, but being apart that long hurts right here," she didn't mean to whine but whine she did. It was sort of a reflex.

Kim dragged a small pillow to her lap and squished it. "We can't adopt you, India. And you'll be fine on your own. Now listen close and listen well," she hit the pillow pointedly. "While I'm gone, you're going to focus on self-improvement. I'm not saying you're not amazing how you are, but I think taking part in self-development activities like yoga could really keep you busy. Oh, and what about what I said? You should join a club! A book club. I used to be in that."

"I know, but they already got a replacement member. Adding me would be a crowd. Plus, I don't want to get close to my sister and her friends. It feels desperate," India bit the last of her treat and crushed the wrapper. She tossed it on the cluttered center table. Cleaning would come later. "Even if I am."

Kim had already finished her chocolate bar. The crumpled

wrapper lay next to two cans of soda. "Your sister and her friends are great," when India moaned, Kim smiled, hugging the plush red pillow. It matched India's living room aesthetic. Brown furniture with red cushions. "I honestly think you'll be fine once you double down on your hobbies. Adding new ones to the list can help too. Who knows? Maybe if you joined the cross country club, you'll meet someone."

"Cross-country?" India grimaced at the notion. "You mean like running for fun?"

"I do mean running for fun. Come on, in high school you loved to run!"

"I was a child, Kim. We all make mistakes in childhood."

Kim laughed.

India frowned, her mind catching on something else her friend had shared. "And what do you mean by 'meet someone'?" Stretching for a soda, she shot Kim a glare. The cold metal numbed her palm as she cracked her drink open. "I've already told you Kim. You and Malik's story was once in a lifetime. And getting to know someone right after leaving Nate feels weird."

Kim lifted her drink next. "I think it's been long enough," she undid the seal, summoning a hiss. "I don't know. I'm just trying to help. It hurts me more than you know seeing you mope about missing me. I miss you a ton too, but distractions help. So please consider some," she drank a few sips. "When you're not working, you can knit or do whatever activity of your choice. And when you're not doing that," she spread her arms as if asking for a hug. "You'll be with me. As in video calling or texting. At that rate, time will fly by so fast you won't even feel it," she raised her can. "Now let's toast to that."

India hesitated, taking in the cheeriness of Kim. Without a doubt, her joy outweighed the dread within her. She'd always known Kim would make it. Since they were kids, she'd been capable. India still remembered those days. Lounging around Kim's house when her mom got busy. Nevaeh would be there as well. She had vivid memories of her sister as a child. Jumping from couch to couch while India and Kim sat below her. They'd have so much fun back then. Talking for ages, fantasizing about their futures. In those times, she'd wanted a husband and five children. The thought made her laugh. Whether or not Prince Charming sauntered into her life didn't matter. Having fun with those she held dear was the top priority. Whether that be with her bestie or a man didn't matter. But for now, Kim would be AWOL. Off living life. So where did that leave India? Sharing laughs with no one? Mulling the negatives would worsen her pain.

Whether or not she wailed or threw a fit, Kim's trip was set in stone. Wherever she went would be marvelous, and the best India could do was support. So, she'd grin and bear the agony. Not too hard, a lot of her loved this for Kim. And like she said, changes came with life. "Right. Let's toast to time flying fast. By the time we blink, it'll be next year," she winked clownishly to evoke Kim's laughter.

With bright smiles, they clunked their metal cans then counted down. When 'three' came, both sipped their sodas.

Some of India's drink spilled, causing a mess on her sofa. She and Kim squealed before Kim sprung upward. "I'll get the rag," she proclaimed.

Meanwhile, India wiped what she could with her hands. Nothing worked. "Hurry before the ants march in!" she swiped a frantic hand across the seat. Taking Kim up on that idea might be best. But sitting through club meetings sounded unbearable. Perhaps with more time, she'd find better distractions. Please let me find some. At the rate she was going, this year might feel like a decade.

Maybe even an eternity, India realized with a grimace.

No matter what, she had to find something to fill her time.

Because longing to be part of her friend's life was just not going to cut it.

"... *And* put it in the oven for baby and me. Yay," Rashad clapped his hands with bouncing legs. Laughter bubbled from Destiny's lips. The bright peal of a baby's laugh rang through the air, and she reached out, demanding that he keep doing whatever he was doing, and held his arms for support. Gladly, Rashad did so. Nothing pleased him more than making Destiny happy.

His niece deserved the world, and he was happy to give it to her.

Water ran from the kitchen sink as his parents and siblings cleaned up after dinner. He'd risen to assist once the last steak was eaten, but Destiny had other plans. A tap on his back told him what time it was; playtime. This meant chasing Destiny back and forth. He'd caught her by the living room settee and sat in it. At that point, everyone agreed to let him sit out cleaning. If Destiny wasn't entertained, she'd rain hell on them all.

"Ice cream man done playing babysitter?" Hakim walked out of the kitchen, clearly dismissing himself from cleaning, and sat with his cellphone out. He sat beside Rashad and snapped a picture. "The guys want to see my niece. Destiny, look here. Look at Uncle Hakim for a second," his camera light gleamed.

"Woah. That's bright," Rashad stopped shaking his legs and Destiny leaned back against him, wrapping his arms around her waist. "Don't hurt her eyes with that," he frowned at his brother.

From the kitchen, he overheard his dad talking farm business. It seemed the petting zoo was still a hit. Rashad's days of cow-milking were great, but he adored his small ice cream parlor even more. No matter the weather, folks bought ice cream. Even on rainy days like today. Customers hadn't hesitated to express their love for cold treats when it rained. Rashad himself couldn't relate, but opinions varied. He loved listening to them. From old-timers to youngsters, they told tales while buying ice cream. And as their ice cream hookup, Rashad offered an ear.

Though mingling with townies satisfied him, Rashad's number one reason for loving what he did was assisting his dad. The parlor provided a perfect partner for his farm as most milk produce was sold to Rashad. He was proud of that too. He made ice cream from scratch, unlike many of the other ice cream manufacturers in town. While it wasn't easy, it was perfect for their family, as ice cream production was a process quite dependent on milk. And how lucky he was to know its main producer. Their team effort did wonders for the family.

"My bad," said Hakim, shutting off the flash. He snapped a picture then hit 'send'. "Hopefully, Preah won't be mad I took this. The guys have been bothering me all day for pics," he flung a muscular arm on the couch's backrest. At that point, Destiny took interest in his cap and reached for it. The troublesome child put it on and giggled, calling herself 'Uncle Hakim'.

Hakim laughed at his niece. "Ha. You look just like me."

Rashad gently took it off. "You don't want to be Uncle Hakim. He has a big job once he gets back to work," he handed back his brother's hat. "Unless you can play football. Can you, Destiny? Can you make touchdowns for the NFL?" he nuzzled her chubby cheek.

"I play. I play good," Destiny seemed certain, endearing Rashad. Her little voice was a blessing to his ears. Just the other day she'd worn diapers, and now she could speak. Before he knew it, they'd be having full-on conversations. They had them now, but she often got distracted. "Uncle Rashad, tag," she patted Rashad's head.

It wasn't a question, and it wasn't a pat. "Maybe you could play for Uncle Hakim," Rashad muttered. Delighted, Destiny smacked her hand full force against his head.

Rashad winced but Hakim clapped with laughter. In response, Rashad rolled his eyes, holding Destiny's hands. Their parents dried plates and cups in his peripheral vision. Soon, their sister Preah appeared too, speed-walking towards him. "We'll play tag tomorrow. It's night time, so Uncle's tired. But don't worry, as soon as tomorrow comes, we'll play all you want," he tapped the pink bobbles in Destiny's hair. It bound her tight curls to form a small puff. The ideal hairstyle for a princess like his niece.

"This is why people don't believe she's mine." Preah sat on the arm of the chair. Destiny called Preah and she waved ecstatically. "Mwa!" His sister planted a sloppy kiss on her baby's forehead then flattened her own short hair. "You handle her like she's yours," she said to Rashad. "These days she doesn't want to be with me. It's all about Uncle Rashad," she pinched Rashad's arm.

"Don't do that. You're setting a bad example," he said as he danced away from her fingers. He set Destiny between him and Hakim then looked in the kitchen. In there, his dad shook a wine bottle as their mom took down glasses. Together, the old couple shared a bright conversation. Mouthing words he didn't catch. "Are we having drinks before we go?" he heard the rain calming outside. Rain meant food for trees, but Rashad preferred sunlight. It was easier to smile in perfect weather.

"Let them have their fun. What they do in there isn't our business. Even if it is my kitchen," Preah eyed Destiny then Rashad who fixed the child's blouse. Lastly, she settled on Hakim, glued to his phone. "Look at you two," she said. "Just two single Pringles leaching off their sister."

"Leaching?" Hakim sat straight. "Have you forgotten which of us is in the NFL?" he shifted his hat backward and lowered the bill.

"How can I when you never stop talking about it?" she stretched to tap his cheek. "What I meant was leaching off the fact that I was brave enough to have kids," she blew a kiss for Destiny who played with Rashad's hoodie. The plastic blue zipper had her hooked. It seemed so from Rashad's viewpoint. She always looked cute when entranced by new things. "Meanwhile, neither of you have looked at a woman in years, let alone considered having kids with one," Preah continued. "Are you hearing this?"

Rashad received a tap on his shoulder. "Loud and clear."

"Why are you trying to pressure us?" Hakim put his phone down and sat forward. "If someone great comes along, they'll come along. You had Destiny and that's amazing for you, but Rashad and I haven't found someone to settle down with." He stretched a lazy arm over the backrest and smirked at his sister. For an athlete, he sure loved lounging around. Hakim was usually confident, even bordering on insufferable. But, for a moment, Rashad thought he sensed a crack in his brother's bombastic demeanor. Rashad watched him scratch his beard pensively. "And quite frankly, I don't think I will."

Preah sat between Rashad and the armrest. It took much effort but worked out. Rashad and Hakim had moved down to accommodate her. Destiny was back in Rashad's lap. "Why? Because of Jada?" She put up her hand when Hakim tried to protest the question.

"I know that Jada broke your heart." "She didn't break my heart. I ended it with her. Remember?"

Preah squinted. "That's not how I remember it at all."

Hakim settled back, his arms folded. "Then you're remembering wrong."

Preah huffed out a breath. "I am most definitely not remembering wrong, brother."

As usual, Rashad stayed silent between them. Their squabbles were a regular event at reunions. As kids, his siblings fought even more than now. He just thought they'd grow out of it by adulthood. "If you ever get a little brother or sister, don't fight them like your mommy does with Uncle Hakim," he whispered to Destiny. A shouting match was about to commence. "Guys, remember there are children present," his words were ignored, but they toned down naturally.

"Shush, Preah, shush," Hakim dragged himself forward. "You know nothing about me and Jada, so don't mention our relationship," the man wagged his finger at his sister, but Preah yawned, making clear her disinterest.

"You need to get over her," Preah insisted to an irate Hakim.

He bristled, and she frowned. As if sensing his distress, she toned down her ridicule. "Why did you two break up, anyway?" she asked. Simultaneously, smooth jazz came from the kitchen. It floated in like a wandering balloon and stayed with Rashad. He lost grip on his siblings' conversation by searching for its source. His parents had found a radio station to dance to. Watching them melted him. After all these years, the two still shared romantic evenings. His dad held his mom and spun her like a top. Though not seeking it actively, Rashad did hope to one day find love. The love his dad showed his mom. Her twists flew as he dipped her near the ground, and something in Rashad lit up.

Hakim was in the middle of a grand background story. He twisted his beard, looking elsewhere. Rashad assumed he had difficulty with the topic, about what had transpired to end his relationship. "So yeah," his brother ended, reclining. "We were heading in different directions. Two different colleges, different dreams. It was a hard decision, but I had to make it," slowly his body bent lower, like tragic news had been broken. "I wish it hadn't gone down how it had, but ultimately, I had to. We weren't meant to be together, Preah."

Preah made a noise in the back of her throat, giving Rashad the distinct impression that she didn't believe him.

This tale wasn't new to Rashad. He must have heard Hakim

speak it before. Preah probably wasn't around. "At least it worked out. You got drafted into the NFL, and she's doing her thing," he patted Hakim's back through his brother's thin T-shirt. "Woah," Rashad was astounded by his muscles. He drew back and stabilized Destiny. She had started rocking side to side in her own made-up game.

"Have you two seen her around by any chance?" Hakim said casually. Rashad shot a look at his brother. His tone might have been nonchalant, but there was nothing casual about the look in Hakim's eyes.

A laugh from the kitchen caught his attention. The dance session in the kitchen continued. Rashad began to think their parents had planned this, to shoo them to the living room for privacy.

Hakim pulled Rashad's attention back. "Does she still live here?"

For Hakim's sake, Rashad hoped Preah might have met Jada. Rashad knew that he'd seen no signs of her since she split with Hakim. He glanced at his sister who pushed out a lip. "Sorry Hak. She doesn't really come to town that often. And if she does, I never see her," she lifted Destiny out of Rashad's lap. Now, the small child sat on her. As if by instinct, she combed through the frizzy parts of Destiny's hair. Those that hadn't stayed bound by her bobbles. "She was getting a degree in therapy, right?"

Rashad affirmed. "Physical therapy. I don't see her, but the talks are hard to miss. I get the feeling she won't stick around," Hakim's heartbreak couldn't be mistaken. "Sorry, bro. But you know how it is. People grow up and move on. You should too."

"I've definitely moved on. I've moved on so far, I'm halfway across the world. Who says I haven't moved on?" Hakim said indignantly. He flopped back and typed on his cell. "I was just curious. I'm not going to let one girl hold me back from dating."

"Mhm," a sassy Preah hummed. She tapped Rashad's arm, her eyebrows wagging as she included Rashad in her clear disagreement with Hakim's statement. "Sure. We believe you."

"I do not believe him one bit," she mouthed to Rashad.

Rashad would play along, but he felt for his brother. The man seemed stuck. Preah sighed as Rashad shook his head, then her eyes took on a dangerous glint. "Anyway, what about you, Rashad? Is there any secret girl you've been hitting up without my knowledge?" She caught the jazz bug and was dancing with Destiny. They remained seated but swayed to silky saxophone riffs.

There wasn't, and Preah knew that, and Rashad was irritated enough to bite at her lure. "Actually, yes. Today, the love of my life walked in to order a strawberry swirl, and we hit it off immediately," he lied, rubbing his hands. Of course, Preah clocked his mockery. "I'm serious. Have you met anyone? Surely there are tons of single women who walk into the ice cream parlor on the daily?"

"Surprisingly, sis, they're coming in to buy ice cream, not to expand their dating repertoire."

Preah snorted. "None of your attitude."

"You started it!" Rashad laughed. "I mean, isn't that what you were expecting? Sounds far-fetched, right? People don't just meet love interests that way. It only happens in movies," he let Destiny snatch his hand to play with his fingers.

Preah groaned. "Well, Rashad, if you searched, you might find someone."

"I have work," he said defensively. He knew what she was asking, but he couldn't bring himself to do it. At his heart, he was shy, and he knew that. But he also really was involved in the farm, the business, and making sure that his family was at peace. For him, that was plenty. He wasn't a man with huge dreams of being famous like Hakim. Sweetgum had always been enough for him, and it was hard to find a woman like that who came from the town that he also didn't consider to be like a sister to him. Rashad was looking for someone who was honestly as boring as he was, and he hated to admit that to anyone, let alone his sister.

Preah sighed. "You can do other things aside from selling ice cream, helping on the farm, and watching your niece, you know.

How are you going to find your special someone if you don't explore?"

That did it for Rashad. He toppled back in hysterics. "I'm not interested in finding anyone," the lying continued. If someone came into his life, he'd gladly accept them. Rashad did desire love but wasn't sure where to find it. He wanted someone who wanted to be a small-town person, same as he did.

And it turned out, that was less popular than he or Preah thought it was.

Preah threw her hands up in defeat. "Fine. Anyway, let's crash Mom and Dad's little romance session. We need to watch a movie."

Preah stood, and her knees cracked when she rose. "Old age is catching up to me," she laughed. Destiny ran ahead as Preah limped behind her.

Rashad and Hakim walked side by side, both reflecting on Preah's talking points.

"I'm not hung up on Jada," Hakim said to Rashad. "I'm just not dating right now," Rashad replied.

The two brothers looked at each other and sighed. "Preah needs to mind her own business sometimes," Hakim muttered.

Rashad shrugged. "Yeah. I guess she can't help herself. But for now, we're good. Right?"

"Right," Hakim nodded.

They followed their sister to where she was chatting with their parents, and Rashad smiled at his family.

He didn't need someone when he had this. This family was plenty for him.

He wondered how often he'd have to repeat that for it to feel true.

CHAPTER THREE

Stepping out that Monday afternoon should have been refreshing, but to India, it wasn't.

Lunchtime rush. She clung to one side of the street with her final goodbyes to Kim pestering her; their last hug lingering like a heavenly fragrance. She knew she had promised to keep herself engaged, but what was there? Sweetgum was a small town, one that felt even smaller as she contemplated trying to figure out what to do with her time now that Kim was gone.

She had thought of everything available: work, hobbies, that sort of thing. Taking on more work hours seemed doable, but she had scratched that plan this morning. To sit at her laptop for more than eight hours was a horrifying concept. The mere thought sent shivers down her back. Any ordinary person would consider working from home a dream. India had two years ago, but of late, not so much.

For some reason, sitting at home sorting digital documents uprooted thoughts of Kim. It might have been the kitchen setting as they'd shared many encounters there. India's newfound isolation made Kim's absence obvious. When working solo, she had no distractions. It was just India, her furniture, and her mind. Her recent misfortune preyed on her brain, causing depression. She'd almost 'left' work early. The urge to shut her laptop reached a climax.

If only she got along better with Nevaeh's squad. Her nose wrinkled in a cringe. Her sister's friends may have been nice girls, but that didn't mean she meshed with them. Partying seemed their top priority, while India liked getting loose now and then, she wasn't one to carry that energy everywhere. Her sister's friends were the opposite. Upbeat, boisterous, and playful they were. Not exactly her crowd.

She wished she'd been more outgoing as a teen. Maybe now she'd have friends to spend time with. Friends like her who liked quiet heart-to-hearts. Even if she did miraculously find common ground with Nevaeh's group, she'd be a sore thumb. Each one of them was engaged or in a serious relationship, something India couldn't relate to. Dating Nate had been fun, but that ship had sailed.

Once again, she felt listless. Adrift. Like she'd lost all the wind in her sails, and she was just stuck in an ocean, unsure of where to go next.

She skipped over a puddle that hadn't dried up. They'd seen sunshine all day, but last weekend's showers left a mark. As India approached 'Scoop There It Is,' her reflection stopped her. A particularly large puddle near the parlor showed her face. Her heart sank at the sight. Was her gloom so glaring that even she saw it? The water told no lies. That dip in her lips was unmistakable, and those eyes of hers looked sunken. In them was undeniable despair. Just her reflection was enough to get her crying. India's mouth quivered, emotions taking over. Please, she held her mouth. Not in public.

"Look out," a hand snatched her arm and tugged her backward. Instantly, a minivan sped by, splashing up water. She'd been dragged far enough to not be doused.

"Oh gosh," India gripped her chest. She breathed like a sprinter after racing, then faced her hero. "Thank you so much... oh," her dread returned. "Nate."

The sight of her ex-boyfriend really was the icing on the cake of this awful day. Of course, he looked good. Nate wore work attire, something that looked unfairly handsome on him. It wasn't special, just a polo with the name of an establishment on its chest, but he always did fill out his clothes well. His dimples bared in a wistful smile. "Hey, India. Funny running into you here," the man said. Briefly, silence fell as India tried to think of how to respond.

She shouldn't have bothered. Nate did it for her. "I thought you usually ordered your desserts from 'Scoop There It Is' to be delivered." He glanced at the ice cream place ahead. Their catch-up took place by an alley sandwiched between it and Roasted Beans. "Why are you up and about this afternoon? Were you just dying for a summer sun kiss?" his amicable attitude seemed tenfold. But he'd always been sweet.

Talking to Nate wasn't what she needed. His doe-eyes only nailed in her loneliness. Though she preferred staying friends, being around him brought cravings. Desires for the loving touch of someone. It might have been her sadness stirring trouble but whatever it was, hurt. "Oh, I just..." she observed the iconic sign on the parlor. An anthropomorphic ice cream cone spoke the name through a speech bubble. Its scoop of mint ice cream fell from its cone. She'd always found that creative. "The house was getting stifling, so I thought I'd head out," she inhaled deeply, a fresh puff of air filling her lungs.

"Ah, I see. That makes sense," Nate put a hand behind his head. "So how have you been?" since ending things, they hadn't met much. With India working remotely and Nate living across town, the most they'd do was exchange hi's and byes. And that was on rare occasions. When India left her space.

She'd be honest. "I miss Kim. She left last Saturday, and it's been hard," she held the strap of her purse, facing the building.

"She left already?" Nate asked. "I heard about the big-time

producers who scouted her and Malik. I didn't realize they'd start so soon," he beamed. "Tell her I said congrats. It's not often someone from our little town hits it big."

A ghost of a smile came to India's face. "I know. It's incredible, and I couldn't be prouder, but living without her is hard," a cloud blocked the sun, further dulling India's mind. "But it's okay. I've learned to be my own company, so I'll be fine," she just wanted a cold cup of ice cream. Its creamy sweetness never failed her, always providing the right bursts of dopamine. When licking her favorite flavor, her problems vanished. India needed that. For strength. She had work waiting and a year of loneliness to survive. Whatever helped, she'd accept, and ice cream tended to do that.

"I can imagine," Nate hooked his thumbs in his pants' pockets. "If you want, we can talk, you know. In case there's anything you need to open up about. I'm here for you," he spoke with solemnity.

"Thank you. I appreciate that," she shot glances at the parlor.

Nate did too. "You look like you're itching to get your treat," he saluted. "You always did get hangry so go ahead and order your favorite," he walked off with a laugh.

"Ha, thanks. I will," she giggled, thinking back to how sweet he'd be during her grumpy spells. Their relationship was amazing but she couldn't get sidetracked. It ended, and now this was her cross. Combatting depression while Kim chased bigger dreams.

Ice cream was the only way, it seemed, to improve this situation.

Ding! The door's silver bell rang when India trudged in. 'Scoop There It Is' was characterized by its ambrosial aroma of sweet creamy desserts. She appreciated the absence of a line by the counter. Every pink-cushioned booth was vacant. Only employees roamed about with bright lights bouncing off their hot pink uniforms. One jogged past her. A delivery boy carrying a cooler. His pink polo and baby blue collar matched the walls and menu. He greeted her on his way out.

"Hi," India rummaged through her handbag up front. Rattling utensils clung behind the counter where staff members hid. The cashier stood alone, apron on his body. She knew him, and his face was one that was achingly familiar. Rashad and India weren't acquainted personally, but Sweetgumers knew Sweetgumers. This was his shop. His family had a dairy outside of town a ways, and when he had first opened this place, it won some kind of sustainability award, given by the governor and memorialized by a ceremony in Atlanta.

As years passed, he'd tried different hairstyles. These days he wore it short. The look worked. But all hairdos flattered a handsome face. Full, sculpted brows, wide-set nostrils, a notably full lower lip, and dark skin. These features popped out to her. Not to mention his lean muscles and height. The soft apron could not contain his strong build.

But who was she to stand here and study him? She'd never spoken to this man outside of ordering ice cream. He hardly saw her face since she did so from home. Instances like now were a novelty. She didn't want to be a creep, so held back from staring. Though, from day one she'd found him cute.

He was just not her type. India preferred men who were career-driven and ambitious. Serious. For some reason, she liked them to be intense and forbidding, and that was the exact opposite of the man standing in front of her. From what India had heard about Rashad, he could be rather childish. Juvenile? The right words failed but she wouldn't date him. She'd witnessed instances where he seemed to joke and perform for teenage customers. Getting along with kids was endearing in a sense but India preferred her men broody. Not too broody though. A nice balance.

Rashad drummed his fingers on the counter. It was glass and showcased a plethora of ice cream flavors. From berry supreme to chocolate chunk, they had it all. From one end of the parlor to the other it spanned, boasting countless varieties of dairy dessert. They never seemed to end. In her examination, India recognized that a few tubs needed refilling. "Miss? Are you ready to order?"

India heard him but faintly. She lifted her head. "Sorry I just…"

his dark eyes twinkled. As her gloomy mind inspected his face, India forced herself to stop. She guessed this was her loneliness talking. Deep down it was obvious a relationship could not mend her. Especially not with someone she'd written off. Come to think of it, Kim did warn her that being picky would render her lonesome. It wasn't just with men. Friends, dentists, carpenters, India never settled. Could this be the root of her problems? When it came to friends, her attitude screwed everything up. She was well into her twenties and yet so alone. One companion could not suffice. Her nature of work isolated her, and now in Kim's absence, she had no one. Standing here entertaining misery wouldn't help but the thoughts kept swirling like a twister. It took everything to not wail.

While she internally fell apart, the ice cream man's brows knitted. "Is everything okay?" he spread his arms over the glass.

India sighed.

She had promised her friend that she would fill her time with something in her absence. Dating wasn't the best idea because India didn't know who on earth she would want to date.

No, dating was definitely not going to work. She couldn't work to fill her sadness. She couldn't date.

Eating ice cream would have to do.

CHAPTER FOUR

Rashad had worked at the shop long enough to recognize dejection. While ice cream often came with celebration, it was used just as much to dress a wound or ease one's distress. He'd had many conversations with downcast customers who just needed an ear. They often sighed before speaking, just like this girl. Her face wasn't foreign. Not in the slightest. She had grown up in Sweetgum too, but for some reason Rashad knew very little about her. She was local. In high school, she'd been a quiet kid who had hidden behind a book most of the time. As an adult, he didn't see her around town much, but Rashad recognized her as someone who came into the shop with her friend Kim.

What was her name again?

Before now, he'd spotted her through the glass, talking to a man. A man who'd accompanied her to his shop in the past. They'd been a couple some months ago but stopped interacting. He hated assuming, but all Rashad could think was they'd broken up before she arrived. Or seeing him resurfaced old feelings for the girl. Feelings she couldn't act out on because of their status. Whatever it was, he wanted to help. She seemed lost for words due to her heartbreak so Rashad would assist.

He held up a finger and spun to the back. The man held a waffle cone upon return. He whipped out a scooper and slid the glass seal open. Now, Rashad balled some coffee ice cream into his spoon.

She stopped sulking, taken aback by his actions. "Wait, hold on."

Rashad gave a playful smirk. He worked at record speed to assemble her cone. She requested this whenever she called. He couldn't remember her name for the life of him, but he remembered her ice cream order clear as day. They had nicknamed her 'Coffee ice cream girl' due to her preference. He stuffed the waffle cone with freshly scooped cream then considered 'accessorizing' her treat. Formally, one would call this 'adding toppings'. They kept them near the refrigerator behind him. He shook a can of whipped cream then let it rip, turning her cone into a snow-like spectacle. Following that, he picked up a short cylindrical sprinkle shaker. He winked at the stunned girl who waited then shook the colorful embellishments onto her scoop. Next, he opened the fridge and popped out some cherries. "Just like you want it." He murmured to himself.

What was her name? What was…

Ah. That's right.

India. India Carr.

Proud of himself for remembering both her name and her order, Rashad glided back to her. "Ta-da. We know our customers here at 'Scoop There It Is'. For Ms. India Carr, a chocolate-dipped coffee ice cream waffle cone with whipped cream, sprinkles and a cherry on top," he prided himself on remembering it all. To her hanging mouth, he grinned. "Here you go," she must have been impressed. He handed it over.

India took it gently and frowned. "Wow. You didn't even wait," she puckered her lips as if delivering a kiss then ingested a minuscule amount of ice cream.

Watching her face light up rewarded Rashad enough for his hard work. If there was one thing he loved about working, it was bringing smiles to people's faces. Those who'd endured plenty but melted at these tasty desserts brought him joy. A rare joy he could not describe. "Makes it all better huh?"

Traces of ice cream remained on her upper lip. His eyes followed her gesture, and he looked away quickly when her tongue darted between her lips. The gesture made him feel a little… well. It was kind of sexy.

But he didn't want to feel like that about a customer.

She licked it then frowned. "Yes, but it's kind of insane that you jumped right in without waiting for my order," her brown eyes sparkled slightly. He would credit himself for this spark but it didn't seem happy. Was she curious? Slightly annoyed? Whatever it was hooked him. Rashad wanted to know how she felt.

He leaned forward. "Is it insane? Or is it just good customer service?

She arched an eyebrow. "Just because I order this from home doesn't mean I wanted it now. What would you have done if I'd asked for something different?" She loaded more emotion into that single brow than Rashad had ever seen her show, appearing skeptical.

At that, Rashad blanched. She was right. Had he messed up? All the while she licked away. From the cone to the scoop. Her tongue would not stop. He had to look away, or she was going to make him blush. "Oh. I didn't consider that," he tugged his collar then grabbed the counter. "If you didn't want what I was making then you would have stopped me."

"You caught me off guard. I wasn't sure if what you were making was even mine. That was until you were almost done," half her ice cream had vanished.

Rashad had a feeling that he had done just fine on her order.

"But thanks for this," she raised the cone. "Do you remember all your customers' orders?"

The cadence of her sentences felt slow, and that made him curious. If she was upset about her breakup, was she fighting back sadness? Usually, breakups brought sorrowful tears. Would she fall apart once at home?

Rashad coughed, carefully phrasing his response. "Mostly... yes. At least the ones who make use of our delivery service." Her furrowed brows made him feel like he had gone too far. There was a fine line between weird and conscious. He hoped he hadn't crossed it. Establishments who knew their customers were always praised. She only seemed lost because he'd shocked her.

He decided that was definitely why he felt so off, and he smiled at her. "Which aren't many. Hence, I remembered." He opened his palms before resting them back on the surface. "Anyway, has the ice cream helped in any way?" She'd reached the cone.

India twirled her pointy wafer cone then chomped. She wiped crumbs off her face while swallowing. "Yes, actually, but what makes you assume I bought it to help with something?"

These questions. They called him out and made him seem strange. Had she labeled him a freak? Nothing else about her said so. His actions just warranted questions. He guessed he'd be curious if his server made such assumptions too. "I've met a lot of folks who come here sighing just like you." He tapped the glass again. "They're usually in search of a dopamine boost so I just thought you were the same. If that's not the case then I apologize."

She reached the very last bite of her cone and finished it. After chewing, she answered. "It's fine." Small crumbs sprinkled off her hands during her act of dusting them. "You're actually right; I'm here for some dopamine as well." Her sadness returned like a cloud, and Rashad leaned forward again.

"What happened?" he asked before he could stop himself. He was genuinely curious, but after he asked the question, he froze. Was that appropriate? Or was it none of his business? The words fell out on their own.

She gripped a portion of her braids and stroked them roughly, her long lashes batting. He'd never seen light brown eyes so radiant. The pulsing sadness must have done something to them. "My best friend moved away and won't be back for a year. Chances are she'll keep leaving because it's been like this for a while already. I know I should get over it but it never hurts less when she leaves." She sighed. Not once did she look at him. Every ice cream flavor seemed more appealing than his face. It was only after heaving another long sigh that she lifted her face. "Sorry. I dumped all that without warning, didn't I?"

"No, no, it's fine. I asked," he said reassuringly. Internally, he felt a little more settled. Here he thought she'd been heartbroken for a man. Which was worse? Missing a friend or a partner? He'd go with the former. Nothing ached more than saying goodbye to close friends. And it's her best friend at that. Poor thing. Rashad wished he could help. "I'm sorry you miss your friend, but in life - when we grow older, particularly - saying goodbye becomes common." He gained her attention. "But it's okay because we say tons more hellos. As we grow, things change and there's nothing we can do but adjust as it does. Who knows? You might just meet someone who means as much as her in the time that she's gone."

His words seemed to bring agony to the downcast woman. Her lip quivered but she controlled it. With a deep breath, she raised her chin. "You're right. But I don't know if I'll find anyone who means quite as much as Kim."

"Well, maybe someone close will come around." He heard jingling keys as she dug through her purse. Presuming she was searching for cash, Rashad held up his palm. "No. Don't worry." Once again, she stared in perplexity. "It's on the house. Consider it an apology for putting a stop to your adventure by preparing your cone before you made a request." He winked.

She seemed pleasantly surprised. Amidst her depression, she smiled, causing him to notice a freckle near her upper lip. Cute, Rashad thought. She bowed her head. "Thank you."

"It's no problem," he licked his bottom lip. "I'll be prepared for your adventurous streak next time. Don't worry." She'd started backing up but paused to listen. The statement made her laugh before she left. More thanks were said and 'you're welcomes' were given. Rashad smiled as she dinged the bell then whistled low. Nice girl.

He hoped, strangely, that he would get to see India Carr again.

And the next time, he'd ask her what she wanted, instead of just giving her what she assumed she needed.

CHAPTER FIVE

To stop her negative thoughts from running rampant, India had created a morning playlist packed with upbeat songs. While disinfecting her kitchen counters and frying an egg, she'd hummed along to pop melodies from her childhood. It'd been her intention to lose herself in rhythmic bops but somehow, with time, they'd brought back old memories. Flashbacks of Kim dancing in her mother's living room and long bursts of laughter shared between them snuck in like a ghost. The happy recollections left her rigid.

Ugh.

Everything reminded her of Kim. Kim was like a sister to her. Closer than her own blood sister since they had so much in common.

Realizing the jam session's purpose was defeated, she hit pause to try something else.

However, what else was there to choose? She settled in to breakfast, trying to focus on the food in her mouth and her thoughts as she went.

Work, she thought after breakfast. The morning sky lit up her kitchen from the window. She'd changed into sweats and sat cross-legged. On India's laptop screen were pages of work. Her emails had been answered in record time. Shooting a look at the upper screen, India smirked. It was ten-thirty. Meaning she was off to a good start. Kim's absence may have slowed her down in all other aspects but not work. She'd been even more productive than before. This may or may not have been related to seeking work as a diversion from the pain.

She slowed down at typing when it hit like a bag of basketballs. What if being productive ruined her in the long run? There was only so much work to do daily. India would hate to run out of it and be idle before five p.m. It was then her despair would run wild. "Ugh," the woman put her feet on the seat with knees grazing her chin. She wrapped both arms around them. In just two hours, it would be lunch. Could she wait that long? Wait that long to fight her sadness with something sweet?

Pictures of Rashad slowly slithered in. They filled her head like a gallery. His smile, concern, their conversation. In a very dim day, he had definitely been a bright spot, and she found herself replaying their conversation.

Why was she thinking about this so much? India frowned. It was true that working from home was hard on her, and she hadn't necessarily liked it, especially lately. Working alone left her starved of human interaction. Had that been why she had been so engaged in Rashad's conversation?

Then, of course, There'd been Nate before she went in. Perhaps she was so intrigued by the ice cream parlor owner because she had been crushed by seeing her ex-boyfriend first.

However, that didn't feel right either. The more she thought about it, the more she had to accept the simple fact that she had just enjoyed herself.

The day was all a blur, except for that. She had been sad, definitely, but engaging with Rashad stayed with her. "Maybe because I lied," she whispered to her knees. The hanging clock over her fridge ticked like a bomb. Its circular shape reminding her of time's never-ending nature. The sun rose and fell whether she rose with it or not. Whether her friend stuck around or not. She'd be forced to keep going on. Rashad said something about change coming with growth. Even when she'd reached adulthood, she'd continue to evolve. India knew that well.

What an insightful discussion. For someone so perky like her sister, Rashad seemed aware. She nearly used 'wise' but that word didn't fit. He'd chosen his words well when trying to comfort her. What would he say if she told him? Filled him in on her truth? It wasn't as major as she made it but seeing him hurriedly prepare her signature cone was odd.

He was right. It was generally just good customer service to do that. However, it hadn't felt that way to her. She'd felt predictable. Boring. And maybe she was. Her personality had everything to do with this crumbling feeling. India could not entertain herself. Hence, the depression.

I'm not adventurous at all, she thought back to his noticeable stun. The poor ice cream man had seemed humiliated that he might have done wrong. In truth and in fact, he'd been spot on. Just like all times before, India would have ordered her signature cone. A creature of habit she was. One of predictability. Another reason Kim's absence cut deeply. Being so used to having her around made this all the more difficult. When her routines were disrupted, she suffered.

She rubbed her eyes after blowing air from her nose. *I can't go back there.* Not after giving the wrong impression, or trying to tell the ice cream parlor owner how to do his job.

However, a thought began to coalesce in her mind. What if she could prove to him that she wasn't boring? After all, Rashad had vowed to cater to her adventurous spirit. What if next time she stepped in, he whipped out something new? Something crazy just to surprise her?

What if she ordered something that left them both shocked at her choice?

She laughed at that. The idea that Rashad was spending any time thinking about their interaction was just plain silly. *He's not still thinking of me.*

India was surprised to realize that she kind of hoped he was. His eyes had sparkled, and she kind of had the impression that he did want to talk to her more, but she didn't know for sure. It was in his smile as she left. That man would test her.

That settled it. She wanted ice cream, but today, she'd order from home as usual. The walk yesterday paired with their chat had helped her situation, but India couldn't face him.

"He'd realize I'm ordering the same thing, though," she went back to typing, speaking to herself. One thing she loved about remote work was the freedom to be eccentric. No one could judge her for talking to no one. That brought comfort to her conflicted soul. "And if I happen to see him again, he might confront me on it," she selected a full sentence on screen, then licked her bottom lip.

India snorted with a shaking head. Who was she kidding? That man wouldn't possibly put so much into catching her. As long as she stayed away, she'd be spared his criticism and any wild flavors he might force upon her. She imagined a peanut butter cherry ice cream mix and heaved. Luckily, her stomach was strong, so nothing came up. But a sense of nausea did linger. She'd prefer sticking to what she knew.

And now, the clock read twelve. Two hours flew by in a flash. After thinking back and forth about Rashad, she'd worked at a regular pace. Not quickly to bypass upsetting thoughts and not slowly due to gloom. She'd been her normal self. How reassuring? With enough self-monitoring, she'd conquer this hurdle.

Noon meant lunch, and lunch meant dessert; the ice cream she'd thought of ordering. India dragged her chair against the floor's tiles, considering some brief exercise. Getting up wasn't much but it did aid blood flow.

She set sights on the fridge, craving ravioli. Last night, she'd made a pot-full which would serve as lunch today. But before that, she'd focus on circulation. Her legs had gone numb from sitting for hours. This was also why she'd left the house yesterday. Just to stretch her limbs. Taking a walk later wouldn't hurt. As long as she stayed clear of Rashad's parlor.

Knock, knock, knock! "Delivery for Ms. India Carr."

India whirled on her heel in complete confusion. She hadn't ordered anything. With fingers scratching her neat head of braids, she stuffed her feet in fuzzy slippers. "Coming!" hastily, she stalked past the table and hurried to the smooth apartment door. Had she subconsciously ordered ice cream in advance? Timing for orders mattered. Though quick in their deliveries, putting in her request before noon was smart. That way, dessert would be ready before she ate. No waiting required. She'd done so before. Today just saw a different version of her. A distracted version that hadn't thought ahead like normal. Which was why she knew for sure that this wasn't her doing. She hadn't lost it completely. No order had been placed. The delivery man outside must have had the wrong apartment.

"I'm so sorry, but I didn't order anything," India barely opened the door. Her outfit was not meant for perception. Also, letting strangers see into her living room felt unwise. Sweetgum had been labeled 'safe' by all who lived here, but India took the expression 'better safe than sorry' to the extreme.

The danger was more that people would gossip about her answering the door in her pajamas and slippers, and that was possibly even worse.

Through the crack in the door, India's eyes widened.

The delivery person was wearing one heck of an outfit.

A shocking hot pink polo dressed the delivery man's upper half. The logo of 'Scoop There It Is' decorated his left breast pocket. He even wore a cap, communicating clearly to India that this was their delivery man.

She'd half expected Rashad once the colors jumped out at her.

Realizing this, India shook her head at herself. Of course, Rashad wouldn't be out and about delivering ice cream. He was the owner, not a delivery boy!

"Thank you," she said softly.

The delivery guy smiled. "Here," he said, offering her the familiar pink insulated bag. She knew from experience that this was ice cream. She recognized her treat's usual packaging. Did anyone else on her floor order from them? As far as she knew, every neighbor had gone to work. So, what did that mean?

"Um. I really appreciate it, but I also didn't order this," she clarified.

"I know. But the boss sent this for you specifically," with a warm smile, the delivery man handed her the package. "Enjoy your day Ms. Carr," he waved when she took it then continued with his business.

India was speechless. She stretched her neck to observe as he walked but gave up prematurely. "The boss?" she questioned to the empty air.

She could picture the boss in her mind, and she conjured up an image of Rashad's handsome face and kind advice. She thought of these while heading for her table. A twinge of warmth bubbled in her belly and stretched to her limbs. They stopped at her cheeks and sizzled them.

Girl. Get a hold of yourself. You really need to get out more if a man doing his damn job has you all bothered like this.

She walked inside and decided to put the ice cream in her freezer.

While unpacking the cubed shape bag on her counter, India found a note. It'd been strapped to the miniature ice cream tub inside. She wiped stray water droplets onto her sweatpants before reading. He'd laminated the note and everything, keeping water out.

Hey,

I hope you're doing well, India Carr, and that my surprise doesn't startle you. I just love creating different flavors for the parlor. Normally, I taste test them myself, but this time I thought maybe some assistance might help. It works for both of us. I get a second opinion while you get satisfaction for your thirst for adventure ;)

From Rashad

"Wow," she put the note down and blinked at it.

This was weird. Somehow, a prediction of hers had come true. Granted, it was a little different than she'd imagined, but the essence remained. Rashad had sent her a wild ice cream flavor. Another tub sat beside that one with the label of what she'd had yesterday. Seeing it relieved her. How kind of him to send what she loved? But it wasn't this that seized India's attention.

Picking up the cold tub of foreign ice cream, India considered it. She turned it around, looking for the flavor. "I hope it's not gross," she muttered to herself. She sighed as she looked for the label. Why was she tingly? He was just easing her based on their conversation, and she should be mad about it. She read the tub's label with squinted eyes and hummed. "Raspberry Cream Swirl?"

What an interesting combination. She popped off the lid with a subconscious smile and licked it. *Not half bad*, she thought giggling.

She took another bite. The flavors crashed on her tongue, and she shut her eyes, reveling at the fact that they were new. They were good.

They were kind of an adventure.

India put the treat away, choosing to responsibly have lunch before exploring Rashad's new flavor. When the time came, however, she lovingly got the ice cream out and sat down with it. While sitting at the table, she licked off her spoon. It wasn't her ideal type but tasted delicious. She liked it enough. There were at least four scoops in here. While ice cream did entice her, she couldn't have too much in one serving. As far as scoops went, two was enough.

She ingested as much as she could before storing the tub away. It fit perfectly between her frozen chicken and pizza pockets. India swung her freezer closed then sat at her computer. Try as she might though, she couldn't regain her work mindset. This man actually remembered her. He took it a step further to not only give her some thought but to send her ice cream free of charge. What did that mean?

Her phone screen read one p.m. when she checked it. Not even an hour later.

Suddenly, India realized that she should probably reach out to him. Should she send an email to the parlor? He'd sent this for taste testing. Rashad wanted feedback. *But I don't know.* She was suddenly a timid teenage girl. Uncertain and shy.

After crossing her legs in her seat, India drew a conclusion. She'd leave this alone for now. He didn't mean it literally. He didn't want her to follow up or anything like that. Rashad made a nice gesture this one time that would not continue. That had to be the case. Plus, her opinion may not benefit him in the long run. She found the flavor 'fine' but not spectacular. This had nothing to do with his lack of expertise but her affinity to sameness. If she somehow spotted him while on an errand, India would gladly show gratitude towards his gesture. But for now, she'd avoid making contact.

Back to work she went, fighting a goofy grin. How sweet? She didn't want to read too much into it but even on the surface, Rashad had been thoughtful. It was while sending an email that something occurred to her. Once again, she'd stopped mulling over Kim's departure. *Thank you, Rashad,* and he was the reason. If this continued, he just might be her saving grace. *Don't get your hopes up,* this was likely a one-time thing. Wherever Rashad was now, he'd definitely forgotten her. Running a business took focus and drive. A busy man like him had no time to gush over one customer.

A weary sigh expelled from her lungs. Another surprise tub of ice cream would be neat. Just to get her mind off Kim. She hummed as she worked, typing away.

Her thoughts, interestingly, were all about ice cream.

And none at all lingering on her friend.

"Just put them in the freezer with the other cartons," Rashad called out to his staff. He held a plastic bag of ingredients while instructing some employees. Today was experiment day, when any of the employees got to suggest ice cream flavors, and Rashad made it happen. Some of his greatest (and worst) flavors had come out of experiment day, and it was a tradition that he was happy to continue.

That didn't mean, however, that it was easy. The counter was a mess. Food coloring, sugar, flavor packets, nuts, cocoa powder, and more contributed to its unsightly presentation. To Rashad, they added quite a colorful addition to the normally bland back kitchen. When inventing new flavors, he sometimes worked at home, but hearing input from his employees was always better.

It was good timing as well. During the day, they rarely had people come in to the shop. Typically, Rashad saw a handful of customers before sunset, but after five p.m. was when business really boomed. Nothing compared to weekend madness though. His employees would get a workout running back and forth. He sometimes felt guilty enjoying it, but he did. Busy days meant profit.

They had to take the slow times as they came, and for Rashad, that meant today was experiment day.

"You hear what I asked?" he said to the two teenagers who were giggling in front of the shop.

"You got it boss," one of the two kids called, smirking. He carried four crates of milk to the large freezer door. It grated Rashad's ear as they opened it. That needed some oil. He quickly added it to the mental list that he maintained at all times. Being the owner was great and all, but the chores never ended. He breathed out then shook what he held, trying to mix the items inside.

Ingredients flew out. Rashad froze, half covered in cocoa powder and cereal dust. Had he not sealed this bag properly? "Crud," he set it down to wipe his palm. Out front, employees handled orders. Looking through the open kitchen gave a full view. Someone sped in wearing their cap backward to head for the freezer. They saluted him before disappearing inside. As they waltzed out, the crate boys left with them, and in a single file, they left. Until one crate boy popped back in.

"Sir, how's the new flavor working out?" he asked, bouncing inside. He, along with two of the other younger boys, had suggested the new flavor. The excitement in his eyes gave Rashad so much joy.

Rashad gladly confirmed. "Yup. It's still in the trial phase, but if it works, we'll have more options for our awesome customers. You helped with that," he shook the bag relentlessly before winking. "Do me a favor and get me an empty tub from under there," he stretched his leg towards a rolling stove and counter.

There were three in all. One by the left wall, another on the right, and that one- which was portable- in the middle. They all took on a white tone. Silver cookware hung over the moving stove. 'Scoop There It Is' didn't offer full-blown meals, but having a kitchen came in handy. Mainly for cleaning purposes, but ice cream took a variety of ingredients, and cooking them helped.

The young man did as was told. After searching an open plastic bag within the lower cupboard, he retrieved a Styrofoam tub. "That one looks good sir," he said as he peeled off the lid and placed it near Rashad. "What is it?"

Rashad hadn't coined a name yet. He shook a bit more, then opened the plastic. Its scent satisfied him and reminded him of something he couldn't quite name. Thinking out loud, he replied, "Something like Indian Twist?"

"Indian? Like, as in, from India? Is that an Indian recipe sir?" the boy took a whiff of Rashad's creation. It was a creamy brown shade that almost looked bronze. If chocolate, peanut-butter, and coffee ice cream merged, this might be the color. As for the smell? It wasn't at all like coffee or peanut butter. On the other hand, it did smell chocolatey. Like chocolate with salted nuts.

"Nope. It's my own flavor inspired by Indian spices," Rashad began pouring the contents into the tub while his assistant held it still. He knew why he had the name India on the brain. *I wonder why she didn't get back to me yesterday.* He'd looked forward to another visit all day, but India never showed. Had she not liked his fruity take on vanilla? He'd be totally receptive to criticism. Hers especially was welcome. In fact, Rashad had daydreamed about meeting with her over more ice cream just for it. But that was just a passing thought. Why hadn't she gotten back to him?

Don't be pushy, he reminded himself. She needed space, and she had told him as such. She'd clearly stated that these days were hard. With missing her best friend, India wasn't herself. Sweet ice cream surprises couldn't miraculously fix her. Broken hearts needed time. Time and care. Rushing one's recovery was inconsiderate. He'd heard these words from his brother. The guy may have taken the lead on ending things with Jada, but breaking up hurt regardless. Rashad still remembered Hakim's haunted eyes. *Poor guy.* And in terms of India, it must have ached more. He bet she'd spent her whole life with her friend. Living without her now was difficult. And for that, he'd back off and let India take her time with responding.

But when she was ready, he would be more than ready. The young man's nose wrinkled. "Did you put curry in this Sir?" his disgust quickly morphed to intrigue. "I've never tasted curry ice cream."

That sent Rashad laughing. "Bro of course not. It's not the literal spices of India but more like a flavor with a spicy kick," he nudged the kid playfully. "It's cardamom spiced chocolate ice cream with candied pistachio and a honey swirl," he patted the brimming ice cream with a spoon to ensure it fit. The tub nearly overflowed. "Taste some," Rashad scooped a bit for his curious employee.

With a shrug, he licked some then smiled. "Mmm. That's amazing mister."

Rashad didn't need to hear that. The boy's eyes spoke for themselves. "Thanks. I just hope she likes it. I made this based on her name," Rashad slid to the sink and washed off his spoon. He hopped back with a grin then scooped some for himself. "Perfect," he said after swallowing.

He couldn't help himself. Silently, he cheered the flavor. Rashad had done it again.

"Wait, is this for that girl who was here on Monday?" Crate boy asked with a hand on his cap.

"Yup," Rashad sealed the tub of fresh dairy. He eyed the counter, where experiment day's remains still sat. Oh gosh. He had made quite a mess, hadn't he? It would be evil to get someone else to clean this, so Rashad got working. "Her name is India. Like the country? She says she's adventurous when it comes to ice cream, so I thought I'd send her my new flavors whenever I make them. Just to get a second opinion," he'd snatched a damp rag at the edge of the counter. Now, Rashad wiped up his mess. As if by instinct, his young employee assisted. "I think you should bring the new flavor to Joel. Let him deliver it to her like he did last time."

"Oh, right away Sir? Why not let it sit in the freezer a little?"

Rashad snapped his fingers. "Ha. That's a good idea. Leave it for an hour *then* hand it to Joel," India might prefer firm textures.

Rashad liked ice cream soft, but not everyone was the same. "I'll ask what she likes best when she stops by next time," he'd write a note while it froze.

Ten minutes passed with Rashad rinsing a soiled rag. He twisted the pipe shut, then squeezed excess water from the rag. After hanging it on a bar over the counter, he sighed contentedly. *I sent the last one at midday,* he checked his watch. In just two hours, it would be time. Currently, he stood alone among kitchen appliances and counters. His young assistant had packed away what he'd made and shut the freezer. Had an hour passed? *Okay, stop getting distracted.* There had to be work awaiting him outside. India may have intrigued him, but letting her consume his thoughts was irresponsible. He owned a business that required care.

Behind the front counter, Rashad refilled some plastic spoons. Lifting his head expectantly at any 'dinging' sound drove him nuts. Today, the errand boys kept going back and forth between inside and out as new ingredients came in. In a couple of weeks, Founder's Day would be upon them. While hectic weekends left their stock depleted and staff members worn, they brought in great revenue. So, as a means of preparation, Rashad ordered in anticipation of this. They'd have a loaded freezer on their hands soon, packed with products for Founder's Day specifically.

Ding! Another one of the teens he had hired to work at the shop glided through the door with boxes of sugar. She whistled past tables and chairs while Rashad deflated. "Should I put these in the kitchen corner, Sir?" she asked as she stopped by the counter. Her large arms shook from carrying such a load.

Rashad cast one last glance at the front door but gave up on India's arrival. He understood her reluctance, but it would have been nice to see her. *If she doesn't show up tomorrow, I might just deliver the next one myself.* The thought gave him some comfort. He turned back to his employee. "Yeah, you should see a stack of them in there already," he jabbed mid-air with his thumb, directing her behind.

"Awesome," she put the box down and rotated both shoulders.

"Aw man, that's some heavy sugar," she said. She folded her arms and looked at Rashad. "Apart from serving ice cream, what else are your plans for Founder's Day, Sir? Will you bring your niece to the store? It'd be a nice gesture for us workers," she waggled her eyebrows with the question.

He laughed. His teenage employees were always excited to see Destiny. He encouraged it. It was good for them to see the pint-sized terror. He supposed that about now, she was at school. Pre-school, to be specific. *They grow up so fast.*

Rashad sighed. He pressed a button to open the register, did a quick inspection, then shut it back.

The kid, Michaela, smiled. "Well yeah. She's really cute."

Rashad laughed. "I understand the appeal. She's such an angel, that one," he sighed, picturing her adorable face. Somehow, an image of India with the child in her arms popped up. Rashad blinked it away to stay focused. "For me, what's number one on big holidays is running the parlor. You know how crazy it can get with so many excited customers."

"Right," Michaela hefted the heavy box into her arms again. "But maybe one day you should take a holiday for yourself. You know, so you can take out someone special," she giggled while taking a curve. After making it to the back, he lost sight of her.

"Someone special?" Rashad rolled his eyes, dropping both arms. He leaned forward and folded them on the counter. Dating wasn't for someone like him. Between caring for Destiny, helping his dad, and running 'Scoop There It Is,' there just wasn't room for a signifi-cant other. Perhaps if someone incredible showed up, he'd let them in, but to actively seek them? He couldn't do that. Not while knowing how hectic life could be.

Just then, actual customers strolled in with smiles on their faces. *A friend group.* His mood brightened as they spoke altogether, sounding like bees. School-goers usually appeared in the evening, but these kids must have had a short day. *And they chose ice cream to unwind with.* He smiled from ear to ear and waved. "What's up, guys? Ready to order?"

As each kid spoke at once, their words tumbled over each other. He thought of India. By now, an hour had passed. That meant Joel would soon bring her his latest creation. *Hope she likes it.* Exploring new ice cream flavors never felt so exhilarating.

CHAPTER SEVEN

*I*ndia got a rush from this one. She'd never tasted such a perfect blend of chocolate cake and ice cream. There'd been chocolate bar shavings in there as well. She licked her spoon clean while gazing through the window.

Golden rays of sunshine bounced off rooftops below. A delivery truck drove down the street with painted flowers on its trunk. These, as well as its logo, gave away where it was headed. 'Fragrant Flowers' probably had a booth of its own. She'd heard talks of quite a few stands for the holiday. Some of her sister's friends were to have booths as well. My sister... last she checked, Nevaeh's battle with food cravings hadn't stopped. Pregnancy could be a real pain, but at least she was happy. She and her dancing fiancé, Sean, India sighed wistfully then held up her chunky ice cream tub. Sean was great, and she loved him for her sister, but the two of them together were just far too much extrovert for India to handle.

She opened her freezer to put the ice cream in, struggling to figure out where it could go. Finding space for meat and fish had grown difficult in the past two weeks. Rashad insisted on sending daily treats that India loved tasting. This chocolate cake ice cream was absolutely superb, but her favorite had to be the cream cheese ice cream with chunks of cherry chip cake and cherry syrup. She smiled as she remembered that first taste. Rashad's creativity knew no bounds. He never ceased to astonish her taste buds. She dedicated time to finishing each tub on weekends but still had a glut. Nevaeh came in handy in terms of eating what she couldn't, but if India kept contacting her, Nevaeh may want an explanation as to why her sister kept producing amazing ice cream that wasn't even sold in the shop. India herself didn't have that so would continue hiding her sticky situation.

"Mmm," she threw the empty tub out and washed the spoon. India's stomach was full to capacity. Before this, she'd eaten a sandwich for lunch. Rashad's deliveries never missed their cue since they'd started.

She still wasn't really sure why that had happened. For the ninth time, she asked herself, "But really, why is he doing this?" Up to now, she hadn't sent any feedback. India had assumed he'd give up after delivering the first few free samples, but Rashad wouldn't stop. She'd find a note in each package about what he'd made. India considered sending notes back through Joel but never got around to it. To think, these drop-offs were so frequent she learned Rashad's delivery man's name.

"Anyway," India dried her hands and left. She was ready to take the day off for the Founder's Day celebrations. Holidays weren't acknowledged by her work company, so today, she applied for leave. A day off just to hang around town and check out different displays, see the sights, mingle with the townspeople. On days like these, Kim used to tag along but now she couldn't. They'd video chatted last night, but doing so as frequently as she wanted was proving harder than they'd predicted. Kim's days were long, and the time zone peculiar. When India called, she wasn't always available. Likewise, when Kim got in touch, India didn't necessarily have her phone close. They'd agreed to work things out together as time went by.

While tying her braids in a scrunchie, India's deepest fears set in. She locked eyes with her reflection and gulped. What if this marked the end of her friendship with Kim? To avoid her own eyes, India took in her room's reflection. The bed at her back was well-made. Though she'd turned the closet inside out, foraging for an outfit, she still maintained a neat space. Leaving the house messy simply wasn't an option.

"We've done this before though," she said out loud, lifting her handbag off the dresser. She checked her outfit briefly in the full-length mirror. Today saw her in a simple sweetheart top and jeans. She'd tied up her hair to combat the heat. The sleeves of her blouse were non-existent, exposing her shoulders. Like any responsible adult, India had coated her body in sunscreen after showering. The sheen of the sunscreen made her skin glow slightly, and India thought it was pretty, if a little unnecessary.

She left her apartment with a crowded mind, noting that walking did little to help. India clutched on her bag strap while sticking to the left. She alone descended the narrow staircase, giving thought to her concerns. It was true that Kim had left many times, and their friendship stayed intact, but again, this period would be prolonged. India skipped the last step and walked out, letting sunlight blind her. After protecting herself with a pair of sunglasses, she strode down the sidewalk. Kids zipped by with melting popsicles. From here, she heard music on Main Street. Another fifteen minutes and she'd be where she wanted. India would drive, but parking on holidays was a nightmare. She walked leisurely past stationary vehicles, deciding to pay attention to her surroundings. Today was a cause for celebration. Not a time to bemoan her loss. Just like before, she and Kim would be fine. A few hiccups didn't mean the end. They'd fight for more happy years together. A bit of distance didn't mean they were over.

She settled on that thought, instead of the lingering loneliness inside of herself.

‘Scoop There It Is’ was right down Main Street. To get there, she’d have to pass multiple booths showcasing varying talents. Metal barricades were erected strategically to keep the crowds contained on the sidewalks, and to let some access in for emergency vehicles. They encircled a great deal of Main Street. Along both sidewalks were the kiosks. Some were tents, others wooden counters, and a few simple banners raised by two poles. She caught Demetrius, the local comic book store owner, handing out comics to eager readers. Each child happily accepted a copy and ran far with them. It seemed the local toy store stand was a hit as well. Kids in light-up sneakers raced in circles with free samples for playing.

India’s energy spiked as she watched them frolic. Young women about her age seemed fascinated by a makeup stand for a store she wasn’t familiar with. "Must be new," she frowned, wondering if she should check it out, then decided to. Almost colliding with boys zooming on bicycles, she quickly dodged out of their way. On top of their gleeful squeals was music, a pulsing afrobeat medley resonating in the festival air. It blew through two large speakers by a temporary stage taking central position, acting as a focal point for the event.

India sighed, letting herself get into the holiday spirit. Founder’s Day was something she’d enjoyed in the past. Maybe she could again.

“India!” someone called.

India had just been crossing the street from town square to Roasted Beans, which were blocked off for festivities. She’d been standing near ‘Lights Camera Dance’ before taking off. She stopped walking and turned around in search of who’d spoken. “Courtney?”

Within a blue tent before the café was Nevaeh’s friend, Courtney. She was dressed in tie-dye, a colorful blend of blue, red, and yellow that somehow managed to look great on her. She waved sweetly with a welcoming smile and then gestured to the watches in front of her. "I'm clocked in, but it's so good to see you."

India spotted Justin with her, their watches on display around them. A customer spoke with him about one, and Justin gladly provided information. Meanwhile, Courtney kept waving. It seemed she'd hung paintings in the back of their tent. She'd done a few around town when called upon. India thought of a recently painted mural near Sweetgum Elementary. All credit went to Courtney for dedicating time and effort to designing it. "Hi," she finally arrived at the booth.

"It's been ages since I've seen you. How are you doing?" Courtney was all smiles as usual, just like the rest of her sister's friends. Today, a poofy bun served as her hairdo.

As she came closer, India recognized more faces in each booth. Brandi was in a stand with Chris two tents down. The booth on their left belonged to Nevaeh. How hadn't India seen her with Sean? Heck, the coffee shop booth stood beside this one. Practically all Nevaeh's friends were here with their men. Not practically. They are all here. She felt uncomfortable, seeing everyone partnered up while she was here alone. She turned to answer Courtney, her smile a little forced. "I'm doing good. I see you guys have a pretty neat stand going on," she pointed to a watch with butterfly paintings on its band. "This is so pretty. I love the artsy touch your watches have." She admired Courtney's scenic paintings too. If India could paint, she'd never stop.

Justin put his hand on Courtney's shoulder. "She truly is a gem, this one. Sales have been through the roof since we started working together," he lifted the watch India had her eye on. "Want a closer look? We're also working on some customizable watches, where the owner can erase and draw what they want," he puffed out his 'Justin Time' T-shirt in reaction to the heat. "Tell your friends," Courtney just wiped his forehead with a hanky.

India was tempted to respond with 'what friends?' but held the pity party within. "I will," she reassured him. She went to Brandi's tent next. Quite an audience had gathered at the booth beside it. Sweetgumers sure did love food. The other tents were dedicated to tacos and hot dogs. She inhaled the appetizing aroma then admired Brandi's booth. Two moms were here with their kids, lifting books for borrowing.

"What an incredible promotion tactic," said one mom with four novels. "I think giving away a copy when borrowing a series will definitely encourage more reading. You two should open a book store," she pulled her son closer. He wouldn't stop twisting. India aligned her gaze with his. Someone looks like they'd have more fun playing with cars at the toy stand, she chuckled at her observation.

Brandi wore a cap over two pig-tails, matching with Chris who wore a hat too. He dealt with the other mom, showing her daughter a story. "That's a great idea we just might consider," Brandi giggled before aiming that incredible smile at India. "Hey. How you doing?"

India briefly waved then went on her way. Her sister's tent was a hit. About a dozen moms made a ring close by, clapping to salsa music. An upside-down fedora was placed at Sean's feet. He danced away as they encouraged him. Nevaeh, on the other hand, spoke through a bullhorn, telling moms to gather and watch.

Though making a scene wasn't her thing, India fit herself through some moms to approach Nevaeh's tent. Her sister stood behind the counter with a promotional T-shirt.

Seeing so many thriving establishments at once made India kind of want one of her own. Manning these booths looked fun. "Nev," she said, waving to her sister.

Nevaeh dropped the megaphone in surprise. "Hey, it's you. What's up, sister?" She gently stroked her belly. It hadn't grown much since India last saw her, but she liked Nevaeh's instinctive maternal nature.

India appreciated the warm welcome. "I'm okay, but shouldn't you be resting? I know it's the first trimester, but..." her voice trailed off. Nevaeh's last doctor visit had been a little difficult, and

India's nerves were heightened for her sister. However, Nevaeh seemed fine. She held a supporting pole for the tent. Sean continued dancing behind her, gathering quite an enthusiastic audience. Were they really tossing money in his hat? This idea had 'Nevaeh' written all over it. Either her or Sean's cantankerous niece.

Nevaeh shook her head. "Don't worry. I don't feel bad right now, so the doctor said it's okay." She took a deep breath. "You know I'm a tough cookie," she appeared happy and healthy, so India decided her sister knew her own body best.

Nevaeh's smile turned sad. "How are you doing on your first Founder's Day with no Kim?"

Instinctively, India put on a plastic smile. "Better than I thought," she said. It wasn't a lie. She was doing better than she had thought she would.

"Well, if you're lonely, you're welcome to hang with us," Nevaeh shouted, giggling as Sean came up behind her and gave her a big kiss on the cheek.

India did not really want to third-wheel with her sister or her sister's friends. Instead, she thought of Rashad's parlor lower down. Receiving pitiful care from her younger sister did not appeal to her. India had come here to stall from seeing Rashad, but greeting him seemed better than crying over Kim's absence. "Anyway, I should go," she shot a quick glimpse at Joanne's stand with her boyfriend then walked away.

"Wait, so soon?" Nevaeh said through the megaphone. A few heads turned in curiosity. She lowered the contraption with a sheepish grin. "So soon?" She said softer.

India covered her forehead after stopping. She took a deep breath then dropped her hand. "Yes. There's someone I have to see." Would Rashad be available? On days like these, restaurants tended to gather large crowds. He might be swamped with work. But then again, he'd sent her all of those flavors for her opinion. She'd at least try reaching out to him. If they couldn't talk today, then so be it.

Nevaeh tilted her head. "Who?"

Darn sisters. They always could smell blood in the water.

India toyed with the idea of letting her in on this recent development but decided not to. Now wasn't the time. Nevaeh had a booth to man anyway, and a baby to grow. "I'll tell you later. Have fun!" She said another goodbye then squeezed through the crowd to make her exit.

CHAPTER EIGHT

Rashad whistled after checking his watch. The sun was setting, but business wouldn't slow down. It was a Founder's Day for the record books, and he was pleased that it would also be one for his bank book as well. "Keep them coming," he muttered to himself as he continued. He snickered at the register as people filed in. Kids, adults, retirees, all sorts of faces made up the never-ending line at the counter. His diligent employees ran back and forth from the kitchen to the front. They scooped, served, and packaged as fast as possible. Rashad himself worked swiftly, handing out change and storing bills.

"Thank you for choosing 'Scoop! There It Is!'," he said with a smile. He directed a mom and daughter to the ice cream options. The daughter's smile was priceless. Rashad couldn't resist smiling back.

He loved this. Working with customers was his favorite.

After stashing the cash placed in his hand, Rashad snapped his fingers. Joel had just left the kitchen holding a delivery bag. "Flip the sign," Rashad said. Closing was at six. According to his watch, it was about five-fifty. While Rashad appreciated bringing smiles to so many, the good times had to stop eventually. He was getting tired, and so were his staff.

"You got it, boss." Joel made his way past the counter and did as he was told.

Rashad sighed in relief. When these last few patrons were served, he'd call it a day. "Welcome to 'Scoop! There It Is!'. What would it be for you today?" He dove back into work with a radiant smile. These past couple of weeks had been great, but Rashad was never the target for bad days. It could have been his optimistic attitude or a stroke of good luck, but whatever it was, he appreciated it.

He just wished he'd heard back from India. Every day, Rashad found himself looking out for her while working. He continued sending new recipes daily, but India never got back to him. She must have been busy with work or personal matters. He thought this regularly but didn't know the truth. Though Rashad wanted to, he hadn't gotten around to personally delivering anything to her door. He'd been too occupied preparing for Founder's Day and overseeing business. Even if these factors hadn't stolen his attention, Rashad wouldn't have popped up like he'd planned. Sometimes, silence was response enough. India might have seen his gesture as forward. Too forward for her liking. Rashad may have seen his actions as kindness, but others may not. "I just want to cheer her up. But her feelings took priority. If sending ice cream wasn't the way, he would stop.

"Have a great Founder's Day," Rashad said goodbye to the last customer. The janitor was already cleaning up. She wiped off some tables near the left window. He turned to his staff, throwing his towel in the air. "Another job well done, crew!"

Those hiding in the kitchen peeped out with waving fists, and others working upfront gave a round of applause. He directed each person to their assigned places for lock-up then left for the door. There was a whiteboard outside with daily specials. After work, Rashad routinely brought it in to erase. He'd add different menu items to the list first thing tomorrow morning. The ideas were already forming.

As he folded the board and whistled another song, he heard slowing footsteps down the street. They seemed close as they hadn't blended with the buzz of festivities. A hum of music and excitement traveled from downtown's celebration. It was all Rashad heard until these pair of feet came up to him. He noted the painted toenails and anklet before raising his face. His breath caught in an instant. "India," he breathed.

Rashad dropped his whiteboard.

She flinched as it clattered. "Hey," she said.

Rashad picked it up and grinned, hoping she wouldn't catch the embarrassment on his cheeks. "You're here. Wow, this is crazy." He didn't know where to turn. He faced his shop then her smiling form. "Did you come for ice cream?" He tucked the board between his left arm and side. "I hate to break it to you, but we're closed. We just put up the sign about fifteen minutes ago." But he'd make an exception for her if she let him.

Today she didn't look so down. Last time, he'd forgotten to say how much he liked her braids. They curled at the ends. It was hard to see with them tied in a ponytail, but Rashad remembered.

"I noticed." India held the strap of her handbag. "I actually didn't come for ice cream. After all, I have quite the supply at home." She said this with a teasing air.

"Oh." Rashad knew what she meant. He rubbed his head with a dopey smile. "Was it all too much?"

India shook her head, sending her hair flopping behind her. "No. Of course not. How could ice cream ever be too much? I mean, I've loved every one of your flavors so far. They're so creative and delicious," she assured him with a shy smile. "You have a gift."

Out of all the beautiful people to make him smile today, his smile was widest with her. "Did you like them?" Rashad finally received the feedback he had hoped for. She liked every flavor. How amazing? She'd never know how grateful he was for her opinion.

And how proud he was that he met her expectations.

"Yes. I sure did." She clasped her hands below her waist. "I don't think I've ever gotten free ice cream before, so that may have made the taste much sweeter. You know what they say about free things being better. There's just something about them." She looked away. It seemed the sky stole her pleasant gaze. It had gone from a shade of dark blue to light orange in seconds. Rashad himself was captivated. "You don't have to send more samples, though. I think you're gifted enough to know when a new flavor is exceptional." She kissed her fingers and laughed.

He laughed too, pleased with her attention. "I don't know. So far, I've really enjoyed listening to your thoughts." He grabbed the metal door handle but paused before he opened it for her. "Which did you like best?"

India's eyes lit up. She tapped her cheek with a finger. "I think I liked the cream cheese ice cream the most. And your chocolate cake ice cream. But really, they're all amazing."

"What did you think about 'The India Special'?" Rashad leaned against the door, moving it slightly. Would she pick up on the fact that he had made it with her in mind?

India giggled, shoulders jiggling. "Very creative." She took a few steps forward. "Anyway. I should be heading off—"

"Wait," Rashad pushed the door open. "Don't you want to try your favorite flavors? I have some more in the back." He nodded into the parlor. "We can sit and talk over some."

She seemed delighted that he offered. Her eyes lit up, and the expression made Rashad's heart flutter with joy. "Wow, that sounds great, but..." Her thin, sculpted brows furrowed. "I'm a little confused. Why did you start sending those different flavors in the first place?"

Rashad yanked the door open. His earlier elation diminished. Did she think it was weird? Maybe it was weird. He had just been so enthralled by their conversation that he wanted to know more. He wanted her opinion, and mostly, he wanted to make her day brighter.

That was definitely weird. He couldn't tell her that. Instead, he opted for part of the truth. "Didn't I tell you? I just wanted a second opinion." He'd confess his plans to brighten her mood but didn't want to scare her away, or for her to think it was weird. They could talk about anything else but that. "What did you like about my take on cream cheese ice cream? Let's get into it, shall we?" He gestured inside with an arm.

She went in, giving thought to her answer. He liked the way she carefully chose her words, putting real effort into her response. "I like the cherry swirl and creamy cheese taste. Cheesecake is pretty much my favorite treat, so anything based on its ingredients will win me over." They walked side by side to the counter. The closing crew was just about done. She dragged her mop and bucket past them.

"Don't worry. I'll take care of whatever mess we leave," Rashad told her as he motioned for India to wait as he ran to the kitchen. She sat, looking at him hopefully, which gave him courage. As he slipped in, she swayed from left to right, keeping an eye on him as he snuck into the back. He beamed while leaving her sight. Rashad ran to the blocky freezer after disappearing.

He looked at the ice cream case. What would he bring her? He felt pressured to choose something that would knock her socks off. Really blow all of the other flavors out of the water.

Rashad realized that he had sent her all of his best options.

"Rashad?" he heard her call.

The sound of her voice jolted him to action. He grabbed a couple of options, then headed back out to the parlor.

"Okay. These are some of the other options I've got. Let's see how critical your palate is."

India laughed, a chiming sound that made Rashad's face flush. "Bring it on, ice cream man."

Later, India licked her spoon over a fresh cup of ice cream. They chose a window booth and sat face to face. Their two cups sat between them. India's beloved cream cheese was one of them. Rashad scooped his raspberry blast while she had a ball devouring hers.

"So, you're not a fan of digital games at all? Video games are really just a classier version of what you played on the playground," he asked. They'd gone down memory lane together, discussing their pasts and childhoods. Naturally, they wound up talking games; what they'd played as kids. India shared her dominance in physical games, so Rashad asked whether she'd liked digital games too. Turned out she didn't. He hadn't played a handheld game in a while but had enjoyed them in middle school.

"Classier?" Her left brow shot up. As time went by, more employees left the scene. They said their goodbyes to Rashad before leaving. "I don't understand what you mean." She took another scoop and licked the yellowish snack off her spoon.

Rashad stuck his own spoon in his ice cream. "Each digital game uses physical games as its foundation."

"That doesn't make any sense."

"What? Of course, it does. Where else would video games get their basis from? I bet there are some video games that are just like 'I Spy' and the others you like," he said.

India put her spoon down. "Name one." She sat back, partially sinking into the soft pink backrest.

Rashad took a while to form his response. "Oh. I used to play this one on my computer as a kid that was all about locating certain objects in a collection of others." He recalled some good memories searching his screen back then. "It was a lot of fun. I think you would have liked it."

India filled her spoon with more dessert. "I've played games like that on my phone once or twice. They are fun. I'll admit." She tittered as Rashad clenched happy fists. Witnessing her joy sent a rush up his spine. There wasn't a trace of gloom on her face. "But when they make a video game that incorporates elements of Scrabble, then you can call me." India slid the spoon between her plump lips.

"Scrabble?" A surge of joy went through Rashad. "You like Scrabble too? That's awesome." He let go of his spoon. "On family game night, I obliterate everyone at that game. I was so good, my dad made us stop playing it." He didn't normally toot his own horn, but she brought it up. Rashad couldn't let someone mention his game without flaunting his wins.

India looked surprised. "Really? The ice cream man is secretly a Scrabble genius?"

Rashad puffed up his chest. "You thought ice cream was my only area of expertise? Not a chance. I've got tons of talents up my sleeve." He glanced into his half-eaten cup. The A.C. failed to stop it from melting. But in Rashad's eyes, melted ice cream was still ice cream despite its soft texture. "I'd have no problem showing you just how skilled I am. In fact, I bet I could beat you in a game."

India seemed amused. "Really? You think you can beat me at Scrabble?" She had a good laugh. "Back in high school, I once competed in a tournament against our rival school, and guess what?" She arched an eyebrow, cutting Rashad off before he could respond. "I won." India sat back, seeming pleased. "And that was a legitimate competition. Far different from some family game night."

He liked how her attitude took a one-eighty when it came to Scrabble. This side of India was endearing. She was confident and sexy, with an attitude that he enjoyed. Her eyes and face seemed brighter. He'd take this to mean she'd gotten comfortable. Comfortable enough to boast and joke around. "That's extremely impressive. I didn't know they had school tournaments for games like Scrabble. I've heard of chess tournaments, but that's about it. You must have been some kind of grandmaster."

"Well," she said, acting coy. The young lady twirled one of her braids. "I don't think Scrabble has those titles, but if they did, who knows?" She peeped into her cup as if something in it would surprise her. "All done. Wish I had more."

"I could get some." He perched his elbow on the backrest of his seat. Rashad hadn't seen when it happened, but somehow, he and India were now the only ones here. His workers must have left faster than he'd anticipated. They'd been itching to enjoy the Founder's Day festivities. He himself wouldn't mind checking out a few booths but was loving his time with India. She seemed so much better. He'd pat himself on the back for that.

India vehemently denied this offer. "No. I've been eating way too much ice cream of late. Believe me, if there were no repercussions, I'd go wild, but there are, so it's time I took a step back."

Rashad could respect that, even as his heart squeezed with sadness. He watched as she slid her handbag onto her shoulder. They'd had a fun time, but it was getting late. The transparent doors didn't lie. Darkness had fallen over town. Would she be alright walking home by herself? He'd offer to accompany her but had some cleaning up to do. It can wait. "Will you be walking home by yourself?"

India raised her brows in clear stun. "Oh. Yes, actually. Sorry. I didn't even say goodbye yet."

He laughed. "I saw you grabbing your bag, and it's late. Naturally, I assumed you were leaving." Rashad got up, and she did too. He shot her a smile. "I guess with all the Founder's Day celebrations, you should be fine. Unless you need a walking partner."

"A walking partner?" India arched another one of those perfect eyebrows at him.

His grin widened. "Yeah, someone to walk down the street with."

"I think they call that a friend," she laughed. Immediately, he wished she hadn't said that word. Her smile faded, and some of the sadness came back into her eyes.

Rashad didn't want that. He'd worked so hard to get that sadness to leave her eyes. He didn't want to see it there again. "Well yeah. I guess that's right."

"Mmm," India affirmed.

Well, here it goes. Rashad sucked in a breath. "We should be friends." Making new friends came easy to Rashad. He never let doubts stop him from forming bonds with others. Friendship was a gift he absolutely cherished. India seemed in need of new bonds, so he'd happily use his impeccable people skills to extend a hand.

Plus, he did want to be India's friend.

Again, his words seemed to catch her by surprise. He saw it in how India's eyes popped. This stun didn't last though. She looked rather elated after processing his proposal. "Sure. Why not?"

Rashad grinned again. "Why'd you look so shocked that I asked?"

"Ha. It's just not often that someone comes out and says they should be friends with someone else." She laughed, but it didn't hold much humor. "I kind of assumed we already were since we sat down over free ice cream together."

Rashad couldn't deny her logic. "You're right. But I wanted to be sure you knew how I felt since there's something I just remembered that I think you'll like." He rubbed his hands like a mad scientist.

"Oh?" India seemed intrigued. "I'm listening."

Rashad was happy that she was. "In that case, I'd say that we are friends."

He tried not to hold his breath while he waited for her response.

When it came, his heart skipped a beat.

"You know what, ice cream man? I'd say we are. And yes, I'll take you up on that walk."

Rashad held the door for her, ushering her out. When the bell jingled this time, he was happy to hear it.

Because the light ring reminded him a whole lot of India's laugh.

CHAPTER NINE

The air carried the fading scent of a summer day as Rashad and India walked back toward her apartment. India breathed it in, marveling at the dusky sight of the sun as it slipped away under the horizon. Summer nights didn't necessarily mean that the Georgia heat disappeared, but they did mean that there was often a cool breeze nearby. She felt the edges of the breeze ruffle against her shoulders as they walked.

She kept sneaking glances at Rashad. He was handsome. She'd be lying to herself if she denied that. But what was really attractive about him was his charisma. He was all smiles and laughs. Hell, the man made ice cream for a living.

She still wasn't quite sure why exactly he was so interested in her.

But for right now, she wasn't going to ask too many questions. It was a nice night, and she was full of ice cream, and for once, she didn't want to slip back into the sadness that felt a little more distant than usual.

"So, you can kick butt and take names at Scrabble. Any other hidden talents?" Rashad strolled with his head held high along the clear sidewalk. He'd driven them here in one of his delivery vans.

India liked how everything associated with his business came in hot pink and baby blue, like the shirt he wore from the uniform he hadn't changed. India, on the other hand, was dressed in a thin red sweater and black pants. She'd chosen sandals for her feet, and she was kind of regretting it. She hadn't expected to get this much mileage out of them in one day.

But they sure looked good, and she was glad.

"No, not really," she said. The last of the sunlight slipped over the horizon, leaving a rosy glow in the clouds. Normally, she'd feel sadder about this. The sun was just about setting on another day with no Kim, after all. India would normally heavily linger over this fact but oddly couldn't. Her eagerness for Scrabble prevented her. She looked over at Rashad. "I definitely crush a Scrabble game, though."

"You know, Peachwood has a Scrabble league."

"Oh, really?" India mulled this over. She knew little about Peachwood, despite the fact that it was one town over and the high schools were the biggest rivals. She'd last been here for the football game last year, along with much of Sweetgum. Same with the rest of the town, the conclusion of the game had been rather disappointing, with Peachwood coming in first. She hoped that next season, their team would prevail. Losing to Peachwood was just unacceptable.

Rashad nodded. "I know, right? It's kind of like how Demetrius hosts game nights at Nerd Central Comics and Video Games. But only that the league is dedicated to one board game. The one we're both exceptionally gifted at playing," he waggled his eyebrows playfully. "We could have a showdown. See who the real Scrabble champion is."

India laughed. "I mean, I could probably take you up on that."

"It's a date. I'm sure bringing an exceptionally gifted player won't make me any friends, but it will be nice to have a challenge," he winked at her.

"Okay. That sounds nice," India agreed. She tried to hide her exuberance behind nonchalance but wasn't doing quite as good a job as she wanted. If only Rashad knew just how competitive she could be. "Exceptionally gifted." She tried saying it a second time, liking its cadence. "I like that. An exceptionally gifted Scrabble player." India almost crossed the street, but Rashad steered her by the shoulders. She instead took a corner on the sidewalk along with him. This corner had a hot dog stand on it. They swerved around its long line. "Wait, but why don't we have a league at Sweetgum? If Demetrius hosts game nights, why didn't he ever think of creating some sort of league for us?" It hurt knowing they had to leave town for a good game of Scrabble.

She could tell Rashad was laughing, but a zooming motorcycle drowned out the noise. "You know Demetrius. He's more of a Dungeons and Dragons kind of guy. I think that the board games they play at his store are more in that field than classic board games," he said.

"Oh, I see." India should have thought of that.

They talked more about games and how Peachwood varied from Sweetgum. India liked that Rashad shared her views. Sweetgum just had a certain charm to it that Peachwood didn't. They both liked its setup, though. It just seemed bigger. Less cozy than what they were used to.

"It's nice, definitely. But Peachwood will never be Sweetgum." Rashad had walked her to the block where Roasted Beans was located. "I like the pastries here. Hope they're as good as back home." He skipped forward, inviting her to follow.

India simply jogged to catch up. When they entered the cool café, her mouth popped open. "Wow, it's pretty busy in here, isn't it? Not a booth stands empty. The line upfront is just two people but only because everyone else has found a seat. How nice? Nevaeh's friend Joanne saw success here too. India didn't know Joanne that well but had picked up on a few character traits. That girl worked hard for what she wanted. These incredible results were certainly deserved.

"Yes, I heard Peachwood really likes Joanne's coffee." Rashad went to the line and waited. "Think they'd like my ice cream?" He asked with a joking attitude.

India smiled and gave a sure nod. "Of course, they would. If you're willing to start from scratch in a new town." She liked encouraging others. Encouragement always pushed her to face her fears so India made sure to give people that nudge too.

"I'll think about it." Rashad's pep seemed unbreakable. She hadn't known him very long but realized his optimistic nature. She liked it. At a time like now, India needed that. With Kim being gone and all.

They met both Joanne and her boyfriend when it was their turn to order.

"India. Hi. What are you doing here at the festival?" Joanne had on the Roasted Beans polo and cap. She matched with the baristas and manager. His nametag read 'Xavier' and was stuck to his apron.

Her confusion made India's heart squeeze. Was she really so much of a recluse that it was shocking to see her out and about? She shot a glance at Rashad, hoping that he didn't notice the other woman's shock.

"Rashad was just telling me about the Scrabble league over in Peachwood."

Xavier looked enlightened. "Ah, so you've come to spend time with our top Scrabble players. I see, I see." His short sleeves revealed strong arms. The man folded them pridefully. "I hope you two are in for quite the competitive night. Our Scrabble league is top-notch." He winked.

India exchanged looks with Rashad, who shared her unimpressed expression. "We'll see about that," she said.

Joanne seemed mildly weary of Xavier's boasting. She flicked his shoulder, to which the man reacted confusedly. Watching them hiss back and forth made India giggle. Rashad looked pretty entertained by them too. In the end, Xavier gave an apology for showing off. It wasn't much of an issue, but they accepted it.

"Anyway, we're getting sidetracked. What are you guys having today?" Joanne was all smiles again.

Once Rashad had his cookie, they went on their way. He'd bought something for India too. She'd insisted he didn't have to, but he'd done so anyway. As they shared their pastry, India and Rashad discussed past winning Scrabble strategies. India had more than Rashad since she'd played more in high school. He gladly lent an ear as she described her greatest wins.

India laughed. The peer pressure was getting to her. "Okay. I get it. I'm in."

Rashad's eyes twinkled. "It's definitely a date then."

India pretended her heart didn't leap at the thought.

THE NIGHT of the Scrabble game somehow came too soon and not soon enough at the same time.

When Rashad picked India up, she tried not to be awkward. She wore a pretty dress, and it ruffled in the breeze as he helped her up into his truck.

"You look like you're ready to mix some letters into oblivion," he grinned at her. "A dress that pretty is a good diversion tactic. You're doing a great job of distracting me, if that was your goal."

"I guess you'll never know... until it's too late," India smiled at him.

India liked that he hadn't commented on her appearance first. They chatted about nothing in particular on the ride into Peach-wood. Rashad made her laugh when he talked about the teens he had hired at the shop, and she commented on some of his new flavor ideas.

When they pulled up to the central Peachwood library, Rashad helped her down from his truck. His hand was warm where it touched her, and it sent a shiver of something fluttery through her stomach.

Walking in, Rashad gave her one of his signature grins. "Aren't you scared that I'll use everything you've told me against you this evening? Because if given the chance, I *will* defeat you, India." Rashad raised a fist as they entered the double library doors. A banner hung from an upper railing ahead. Below it, groups congregated at tables covered in Scrabble pieces. It didn't seem they'd started. Someone at the front desk nearby dealt with new arrivals. They handed two girls some tickets and sent them off.

India followed Rashad as he went to get them tickets of their own. "I can tell you're good, but there's no way you can master anything I described between now and the games." India stopped when he did.

"Here for the tournament?" The librarian stuffed her hand in a bowl beside her computer then handed them two red strips of paper. She also lifted a black plastic bag and asked them to dip.

India went first. "This will determine who we play?"

"Yes. It most certainly will. Let's hope you don't get a pro for your first game." The woman chuckled and tossed the bag to Rashad after India drew her slip.

India scratched her head at the number on her paper then waited for Rashad to read his. "You know Peachwood better than I do. Do you understand how this works?" She thanked the librarian for assisting them then moved past a few bookshelves until settling elsewhere. They chose a spot near some older women encircling a table up front. The women's position made them seem important. Judges perhaps? *Then we're in the right place,* India thought. India tapped one of their shoulders while Rashad scanned his slip.

"Slip, please," one lady requested.

Rashad handed his over after India. "My guess is that whoever got the same number as us is who we play for the first round. But I could be wrong. I've never played Scrabble here." He admitted sheepishly. They were told where to sit, and soon, the tournament commenced.

India shook hands with her opponent at a table beside Rashad's. There were six tables in all, each holding six players. She lined up her letters when they were given, then considered an abundance of word combinations. Her opponent, a chubby old man, went first and she quietly watched what he spelled. *Car.* How sweet of him. She thought of four different words to form around those letters.

"Take your time, little lady," the jolly old man clasped his hands. He had a thick gray mustache.

"Trust me, sir. There's no need for me to do that." She used his 'r' to spell 'rise' then sat back. While he assessed his allotted letters, India checked on Rashad.

She definitely wanted to get the easy matches over with, so that she could move on to the bigger fish.

Rashad had struck up conversation with the teenage girl he played against. That was until she spelled something that silenced him. India couldn't see the word, but the girl's smirk paired with Rashad's reaction was telling. If Rashad wanted to win, he'd need to put his laidback attitude aside. Deep down, India really hoped to play him; a nice match one on one. But if he got booted before that, they'd be denied this wonderful competitive scene for their first face-off. She wouldn't mind inviting him over, but nothing could replace the thrill of a tournament.

Don't mess up, Rashad, she thought. The old man just spelled 'ice' with her 'i' and India was already playing. She formed the word 'me' with his 'e,' and things got heated from there.

A surge of relief went through her when Rashad won his match. Obviously, India won hers and shook hands with her adversary. Next, she and Rashad went against other winners. Both judges and losers watched in amazement as they used sheer intelligence to conquer yet another pair. She gave her full focus to this match since Rashad proved his capabilities. Now, with a shrunken number of competitors, they were instructed to sit at one table. India sent a smile to Rashad who returned it full force. They sat facing their opponents with determination. About an hour had gone by already.

Two more passed before the semi-finals came along.

India hid her confidence while finishing up her match. The fascinated eyes of both the judges and former players made this ten times more enjoyable than it would be on its own. She and Rashad sat side by side, exhibiting great skill at building words. At one point, she'd received applause for cleverly assembling 'thanks' with limited options. By now, everyone here respected her, but India didn't play for glory. She just loved that sweet satisfaction of spelling words under pressure. It really challenged her mind.

"No!" said Rashad's opponent. "What are you? Some kind of professional?" He grabbed his head in defeat.

Rashad hopped up and executed a short dance. He grinned at India after finishing, relishing in the applause from onlookers. "Looks like we'll be the finalists if you win." A dirty glare was shot to him by the boy facing India. "I said 'if.' I'm not doubting your skill, man." He sat down as everyone who'd been invested in his game switched to India's.

India giggled at Rashad's nonchalance. She put a shush finger to her lips in response then went back to finishing her game. "You've been great, but it's getting kind of late." She spelled her final word with the rest of her letters then rejoiced with squeals.

"Aw man," said the teenage boy. He sighed but reached out to shake her hand.

India commended his efforts while the assistants cleaned up what she'd left. She smiled at Rashad who held his thumb up. His face changed when he flipped it upside down, sending a message to India. She only rolled her eyes and fanned him off. He'd get what was coming when they played in just a few minutes.

Even ordinary library-goers gathered to watch. They fit within the ring around her and Rashad's table. Having this many spectators filled India with life. She could do this. No doubt about it. Rashad was better than she'd imagined but not better than her. As long as she stayed focused, she'd win.

Just ten minutes in, their board was crowded. It was Rashad's turn, and he wore a sly grin. The man rubbed his hands as if scheming. "Sorry, India, but there's no way you can come back from this. These here are some of my last letters, and I already know what I'll use the very last one to spell. You were tough, but we both knew who'd win when it came right down to it." He laid his letters in front of a 'g' she'd used to spell 'giant.' His word was 'coming' and quite strategically placed.

Whispers rose as India shut her eyes in response. Brilliant. He'd played brilliantly just now. "You were sitting on that one for a while, weren't you?" she asked, sizing up her options.

Rashad sat back and brought his chair with him. He balanced on its two back legs. "I've honestly just been going with the flow."

"Oh yes. I *definitely* noticed." India grinned with fake mischief. She picked up some letters, and his face started dropping. "But while you've been letting your natural knack for this game run the show, I've been planning and observing." She didn't mean to go full-on cartoon villain but couldn't help it. The crowd seemed absolutely enthralled by her next move. The 'o' in his last word and 'l' of another fit perfectly. She'd been meaning to get rid of this 'v.'

India spelled 'lovers' using her last letters and others on the board. When the judges saw that she'd finished, they deemed her victorious. Resounding applause followed. Spectators praised her sharp mind, and she received a blue ribbon. Rashad got one too then held out a hand.

She shook it. "You were *really* good." They basked in the praises then shared a laugh. Snacks were distributed outside. Rashad looked them over, then turned back to her.

"How about we get something a little more substantial?"

India nodded. "I'd like that."

❀

"I'M TELLING YOU. You might have an above-average IQ," Rashad said. The crescent moon shone like the stars around it. With these and Peachwood's streetlights shimmering radiantly, they had plenty of light to navigate the sidewalk.

India's self-esteem hadn't been boosted in a while but that tournament did the trick. She could move a mountain right now. "I don't think a high IQ has anything to do with it." She hadn't finished her juice from earlier. They'd gotten cupcakes and sandwiches as their dinner, at Rashad's insistence that both vendors were excellent. Rashad had made many friends as well. She'd mainly stuck by his side but added her piece to varying conversations when asked. It amazed her how easily he gelled with others.

"Don't be modest. Come on. I bet you didn't even try to beat me back there." Crickets chirped in hedges nearby. They'd reach Rashad's van soon. She recognized certain landmarks from before.

India stared at zooming vehicles then shrugged, smiling shyly. "I've just had a lot of practice. That's all." The fresh night's air was a blessing after focusing for hours. Today had been warm but tonight wasn't. She appreciated every lick of breeze that brushed her skin.

"If you say so." He backed off. "So, how would you rate Peachwood after spending an afternoon here?" Rashad held his hands behind him.

"Gee, I don't know." India looked around. "Everything seems bigger here. Bigger streets, buildings, libraries. It's nice but Sweetgum's cozier." She'd concluded this already but in her own mind. "I guess I'm biased. Most people like bigger towns."

Rashad seemed thoughtful. "Would you like a bigger town that's not Peachwood?"

"I don't know. I don't really get out much. This is the farthest I've been from home in years," India confessed. "But I bet someone like you travels a lot. You strike me as adventurous." She sipped the rest of her drink, deciding to dispose of her trash at home. There were no street bins in this area.

Rashad rejected this. "How could I be when I have a shop to oversee? I can't just go wherever I please. The parlor requires my undivided attention. Owning a business is a lot of work."

India could imagine. "You don't take vacations?"

"Okay, yes, but when I do, I somehow end up getting busy with work again." Rashad put his hands in his pockets. "That must make you the more adventurous one between us. I haven't forgotten your complaint, you know. When I tried to predict what you wanted and wound up killing your thirst for something exotic."

India's cheeks got hot when he cackled. As Rashad apologized, she forced a laugh of her own. If only he knew. "Seems I've scarred you for life. I promise it's not as big a deal as you think. I still enjoyed what you'd whipped up. Plus, don't forget that you made it up to me by sending countless free samples." The gesture still amazed her. "I can't believe you went out of your way like that. All for a second opinion." She watched as their feet tread the concrete sidewalk. "I still don't know what to make of it but thanks again. If I didn't know any better, I'd think that you—"

"Oh, we're almost there." Rashad cut her off to jog towards his truck.

India was glad they'd found it. Eight p.m. had passed and the drive home would be long. They both had work in the morning. Staying out late wasn't wise.

She buckled her seatbelt and sat back while Rashad drove. He told funny stories as they traveled, the road back to Sweetgum.

India got every punchline. More than that, she noted that when he found something that made her laugh, he found something else related so that the trend continued. *He's definitely a funny guy*, she thought. They cruised through vacant streets as he went on. Peachwood wasn't Sweetgum, but she'd loved being here with a friend.

And for the first time in ages, the thought of having one who wasn't Kim didn't feel quite so terrible. Rashad was a great friend.

India felt lucky to have him.

CHAPTER TEN

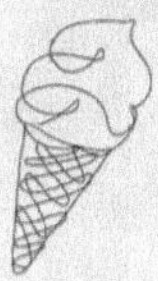

The 'India Delight' was a success. Rashad had made it a 'special' for the first time since coming up with the flavor, in order to test the waters with customers. New flavors didn't always hit at the ice cream shop since regulars gravitated to what they knew and loved. Some went as far as to order 'the usual' when stopping by, and Rashad and his team knew every time what that meant. It was hard getting them to consider daily specials, but despite all odds, today's new addition got to shine.

Today, however, there were a ton of customers who decided to try something new. And, overall, the new flavor was a hit.

"Busy tonight," Michaela commented as she rushed back to grab another tub of everyone's new favorite flavor.

"It must be because that elementary school soccer team decided to mourn their loss here," Joel replied. He had just returned from a delivery about ten minutes ago. He'd usually make his last trip around noon, but today, a request for one large tub of chocolate ice cream was made just an hour ago. His absence during the 'evening rush' had put a strain on staff.

But we survived. Rashad rubbed his neck, recalling the chaos of earlier. Everyone was packing up. The cleaner just rolled her mop pail past the counter. They hadn't closed yet, but at this time, most potential customers had made it home already. The chances of seeing new faces were slim. "Yes, probably. Those kids were wild, but at least having ice cream cheered them up." Sweetgum's junior soccer club may have suffered a crushing loss, but at least Rashad's new flavor got some well-deserved love. And just like the person after whom he'd named it, 'India Delight' deserved loads of that.

Their last outing wouldn't leave his brain. The night had been fun for a variety of reasons. Rashad loved getting out of town, meeting new people, and playing Scrabble. But the thing that had really been worth it to him was her.

India had been the best part of the night, hands down. It had only been a week ago, but Rashad craved more quality time with her. Since then, India made a point of stopping by his shop. They'd catch up on his breaks and hop from topic to topic. She'd proven to be more of a listener but with enough coaxing, would share a lot. He now knew her favorite shows and movies. They both loved action and comedy. He'd proposed they have a movie date sometime soon, and she'd agreed. 'I'll think about it' had been her response, and Rashad took that as a 'yes'.

What he loved most about getting to know her was discovering her loose side. It didn't come out much, but Rashad had caught glimpses now and again. Like when he'd bring up her impressive victory at Peachwood. She'd first behave shyly before holding up her chin to boast as a joke. He liked her laugh and when she fooled around but would never force India to behave in a way that brought on discomfort. When she laughed with him, it was because she'd eased up in his presence. He knew that. She'd called him 'friend' on many instances.

Yesterday came to mind when India received a call. 'I'm just with a friend...' she'd said. He thought of how she'd smiled on those words. They'd been face to face at a booth here that time, sharing views on a new sandwich truck making waves in town. It wasn't revolutionary or earth-shattering, but the fact that she called him her friend, when not so long ago she had been absolutely devastated that her friend Kim wasn't around, made his night.

Rashad felt guilty, though, because while he was happy to call India his friend, he wanted much more.

Being friends was his idea. But he'd always known he'd wanted more the second she'd walked into his life. Ignoring it had been easy when they first interacted, but these constant meet-ups made everything clear. Rashad liked India more than a friend. Her beauty and personality enamored him in indescribable ways. Initially, he hadn't been sure if she was just an infatuation, but now, he knew. Enough time had passed for him to make the distinction.

Confessing his feelings would be anyone's next move, but Rashad couldn't. India was still in a shaky place. With missing her friend and still getting to know him, she had a lot on her plate. Not to mention her reserved nature. A confession might turn her off from new people entirely. They may have hit it off quickly, but it'd still barely been a week. Dropping something so heavy now would break their momentum. And Rashad wasn't ready to say goodbye to their relationship. Platonic or not.

Rashad flipped the 'Open' sign to 'Closed' before stepping outside. India hadn't shown up today. He hoped she was okay. *I'll call her.* He lifted his white folding board with an air of content. Tomorrow, he'd add India's preferred flavor to the specials list. If patrons liked it, he'd officially make it a regular on the menu. "Same with 'India Delight'," he said to himself.

"Wait!"

Rashad perked up when a familiar face appeared in the early twilight. "Look who finally decided to show up." He grinned from ear to ear.

India bent forward to catch her breath. She wore shorts and a tank top. It looked like she'd been running for some time. "I wanted to visit earlier but work had me caught up." She straightened herself and wiped her forehead. "But it looks like I came just in time." Today, her braids were styled in a neat bun on her head. Allowing

Rashad to see her face clearly. "Or am I too late?" After peeping at the 'Closed' sign, her face soured up. "I *am* too late, aren't I?"

"The fact that the sun's already set should have told you." He chuckled while staring at the darkening sky. "It's after seven p.m."

She kicked the ground in evident disappointment. "Aw man. And here I was looking forward to beating you in an ice cream eating contest." India crossed her arms with a sigh then shrugged. "Oh well. Until tomorrow then."

"Wait, no." She couldn't leave now. Not when he'd looked forward to seeing her all day. He absolutely would not let India take off that fast. "If you want ice cream, you can have some. We've hung out after closing before." He winked. "Don't forget who's boss around here."

India hit the side of her head, having a 'duh' moment. "Of course. How could I forget?"

Rashad opened the door to let her in.

Fifteen minutes went by before they had the shop to themselves. Before leaving, many of Rashad's employees had flashed him knowing glances. Joel even gave a thumbs up. Rashad had quickly shooed them off when they did so. If India had seen their odd behavior, she'd suspect something. Something Rashad had no intention of bringing up soon.

"How do you come up with these?" India licked her spoon clean in their signature booth. They'd sat here every day she came. He didn't know about her, but Rashad preferred this side booth because of its seclusion. When sitting here beside the rectangular window, he felt exclusive. Like he and India were alone on earth. Times like now when his employees weren't present made it all the better. They alone existed in Rashad's haven of ice cream.

He slid his empty Styrofoam cup aside, trying to ignore the way her sight of her tongue made his insides shake. They'd just had a sample of something he'd been working on, and he had asked her for her opinion. He was being a terrible friend if all he could think about was how pretty she looked eating ice cream. "It's not that hard. All I have to do is think of tastes that complement each other, then mash them together."

She rested her spoon sideways along her cup's mouth. "But how do you automatically know what works? I would have never predicted that blueberries and coconuts would taste so good combined, but they do. This ice cream is proof. Do you get inspiration from dreams or something?" Her eyes widened in awe. Their light shade mesmerized him for a second, delaying his response.

"Dreams?" The question only struck him as odd when he repeated it. "No, it's not like that." He folded his arms on the table as she continued to guess.

"Is it just a feeling you get?" India scooted to the edge of her seat. He wished this pesky table wasn't here to separate them. Otherwise, she'd be much closer.

Rashad moved to the very end of his cushion. He swung his legs so they hung out of the booth. "I just think that after so many years of working with ice cream that I've developed a knack for it. Kind of like how musicians can tell what chords go well with each other." He got up and took their empty cups with him. "You can be an ice cream master too if you try. Or if you care enough to." His heart skipped a beat when she gasped. He'd never seen her more intrigued. It was cute.

India stood in front of him. "I'd honestly love to but you already waste so many ingredients on me." She wrapped a loose braid back in her bun. Her joy dimmed as she grabbed her hip. "I feel like I'm going to impact your bottom line." She smiled then folded her hands as if anxious, her lips shaking. "Every time I come here you give me free dessert. I wouldn't want to kill your business."

Rashad laughed. "You didn't tell me you were a comedian too." He walked to the counter and lifted a section.

While India stood uncertainly at the booth, he beckoned gently, insisting she follow. "If serving you free cups of ice cream would kill my business, then my business wouldn't stand a chance. Free samples now and then don't do as much damage as you think. Not with the number of customers I see daily."

She lowered her chin while dragging her sandal-covered feet towards him. That shy smile remained on her face. It seemed embarrassment had blended in. He hadn't meant to evoke this response. Should Rashad apologize? "Are you sure? Because sometimes I feel a little guilty letting the boss give me free cups," she said.

Rashad let her go in before him. He fit the movable compartment back into the counter then joined her behind it. "Well don't. The boss knows what he's doing." He rotated his shoulder while leading her forward. "Plus, in this case, I'll be using whatever we whip up back here as part of the menu. We can call it 'India Delight Part Two'!" Rashad stopped in the kitchen doorway to strike a pose. His arms were wide open and so were his legs.

India jumped back at the suddenness of his actions. When her stun subsided, she started giggling. "India Delight Part Two? What happened to part one?"

His heart cracked a bit but Rashad kept it cool. He sighed as they went into the brightly lit room. The ongoing hum of the freezer jumped out at him. He'd need to go in there for some ingredients. "If only you'd come earlier. You would have seen what a hit it was."

He heard her follow him to the large metal door. "Wait did you put that ice cream on the menu today? The one with the—"

"Yes, I did." Rashad dragged the freezer open, inviting clouds of vapor to blow out. He loved how it tickled his warm skin. Even with the air conditioning on in his parlor, the summer heat still got to Rashad. He turned to his side where India had settled. She seemed more refreshed than him. "It's crazy how even at nighttime the heat is insufferable."

India nodded profusely. "Tell me about it. I've lived in Sweetgum all my life and sometimes I'm still blown away at just how dang hot it can be." She took in every shelf and box ahead of them. "Wow. So many fruits and ice cream tubs. This is where the magic starts?" She went in and held her shoulders. "*Brrr* it's freezing."

He laughed at her reaction. "Hence why we call it the freezer."

His polished shoes tapped the rough tiles as he entered. Rashad made an arm gesture to everything then patted India lightly on the back. "Now go crazy. What in here do you think would make an unforgettable ice cream flavor?"

She shivered, still rubbing her arms for warmth. He recognized her thinking face from when they'd played Scrabble. The woman's eyes shot in several different directions before she said something. "Take those grapes and cherries on that shelf right there. Oh- and the yogurt too. Do you have candy?"

Rashad had already started yanking ingredients off shelves. His right hand was full of fruit-filled bags. "Of course. We're also a candy shop you know. And don't forget our infinite toppings supply." He knew she'd enjoy this. India possessed an astoundingly intelligent mind. He'd drawn that conclusion in Peachwood; after she beat everyone at Scrabble so effortlessly. *She must have been top of her class back in school.* Thinking this only served to further bewitch him. "We have tons of those in the fridge outside."

"Well, let me get them. This is going to be the best ice cream you've ever had." India walked backward then whirled to leave, making Rashad beam. She sure was irresistible when happy.

They'd gathered everything India requested and were now at work. Rashad had whipped out the blender which he gladly utilized when India asked. Unlike when he worked alone, the kitchen counter stayed pretty clean. Whenever something spilled, India would wipe it. Even now as she experimented with food coloring, no messes lingered. Rashad admired her carefulness while cooking. He could learn a thing or two from her.

"This is the part where we pour it in. From here, we let my handy contraption do its magic," Rashad said in reference to his ice cream maker. Now, he watched India transfer everything from the blender's spout and into the machine. Normally, when preparing original flavors, he'd use a more hands-on method, but Rashad reserved the best for India. She'd been thrilled when he mentioned his trusty ice cream maker. He couldn't disappoint her by not pulling it out.

"Be careful!" India used a spatula to steer the blended contents back on track. A large sum had almost fallen. "You need to watch what you're doing, not me." She chastised fondly. Rashad apologized right away. "Look," India pointed into the silver bowl to guide him. "You're too easily distracted."

He liked her brief scolding. "Sorry. I'm just having tons of fun." It took a lot from him to look elsewhere. Since they'd started, she'd been all he saw. Her focus on maintaining cleanliness, her ecstatic hops when something went her way, and her great command of the kitchen. Her enthusiasm was precious to him because it was so rare. He knew that if India was interested in something, she wasn't faking. She meant it with her whole heart.

That made every one of her reactions all the more interesting to him, and he wanted to study her to find the ones that showed what she liked the best.

"Me too." India used the spatula to ensure no traces of batter were left in the blender. She put it down then smiled at Rashad, buzzing. "So, what now?"

He'd gotten lost in her eyes. "Oh yeah. We need to finish this up." Rashad pressed a button, and the batter spun. "About twenty minutes from now, it'll be ready. It's basically rotating what we poured in. Spinning it in quick circles. I'd explain it scientifically, but as long as the results are delicious, that's all that matters." He watched how she packed up what they'd used. India brought them to the sink and started washing. He went after her. "Washing so soon? We'll need the spatula to pour what we made into our cups."

"Yes. You're right." She scrubbed it anyway then handed it back. "This was so fun. Will the flavors clash? I don't think I've ever had grape ice cream. Did I go too wild? You're the taste expert. Do you think it will work?" She bit her lip while rinsing a spoon, and he could practically see the doubts overwhelming her. *Don't do that, India,* he thought.

"Listen, I have full faith that this is going to be a great batch," he reassured her.

Her eyebrows were furrowed into a little vee of concern when she turned back to him. "How do you know?"

Rashad gave her questions some thought before answering. "We did a lot of taste testing. From that, everything was great, so I think it should be pretty yummy. What we didn't test was the Skittles we added to the batter. But I'm sure they'll blend well with everything. But you're right to be concerned. Grape isn't a very popular ice cream flavor. Most people don't associate grape with ice cream. It's also really hard to make, so that's why it's become uncommon." He tried to hide his pride for having this information. India seemed to hang on to each word he spoke. She was definitely a knowledge seeker. "But I have made grape cherry ice cream before on my own."

India rinsed everything she'd washed and placed them on a wide striped towel spread out on the counter. "So, what I'm hearing is we created an abomination."

"Huh?" Rashad heard her panicking. "No, no. When I made grape cherry ice cream, it was amazing, and from our taste tests, ours was great too, so don't worry." He patted her shoulder in a gesture of reassurance.

India remained silent for some time. "Okay. At least it's uncommon." She shook her hands to eliminate excess water then accepted a towel that Rashad pulled out for her. He'd gotten it from a drawer below the sink. "That makes me creative right?" India smiled so adorably Rashad nearly squealed.

"Of course you're creative." He couldn't hide his mesmerism.

India squinted delightedly. "You don't seem scared of taking risks to me. Why haven't you already added the grape ice cream to your menu?" She finished drying her hands and flung the towel over her shoulder. "Every purple flavor you have is raspberry themed." She walked back to the ice cream maker, which continued churning. A red light indicated this activity.

Rashad was about to say he didn't know when the memory hit.

"Oh wait. My grape cherry ice cream actually didn't mesh well now that I think of it." He cringed. "It's because I'd been too ambitious and added chocolate to the mix." Her wrinkled nose made him laugh. "Don't worry. It wasn't *that* bad. I only wound up scrapping the batch because my sister thought it wouldn't appeal to the masses. Not everyone's as adventurous as us, you know?"

Her eyes shifted to the left as she nodded slowly. "I would have liked to try it. But just one spoon. What were you thinking though?" India barred her mouth as soft chuckles escaped. He adored how light bounced off her pupils and made them seem brighter. "Grapes are sour, and chocolate is creamy."

"You'd be surprised what ends up working out when I experiment." He stood next to her and tapped the bowl of spinning batter. It would be done in ten minutes. "I think that next time we play this game, you should try being more adventurous. Grape is pretty out there since we don't use it that often, but I'm talking pure chaos." He rubbed his hands mischievously. "Something like mango and vanilla ice cream with chocolate chip sprinkles and gummy bears. A madman's dessert."

India wriggled in evident disgust. "What? Ew. Rashad you're crazy. No one would want that. While this may work on the menu, something that insane won't. It'd be an eyesore among other flavors. You could lose loyal customers for even considering mixing those." She visibly shuddered.

He liked watching her squirm. It endeared him. Rashad caught his chest tingling. "It'd just be for fun."

India rolled her light brown eyes. "You're so unserious." Just then, the ice cream maker dinged. They smiled at each other, then swarmed it.

Rashad took the lead on transferring the contents to their cups. "Okay," he turned back to India with the cup in hand. "You take this, and we're going to try it at the same time.

She laughed. "So if it's terrible we can both figure it out at the same time?"

"Just for the adventure of it. Ready? On three. One. Two…" he said three and watched her raise the spoon to her lips. Rashad mirrored her gesture, but his eyes stayed glued to India. It felt important, somehow, that she would like the ice cream that they made together. She balanced a small chunk of ice cream on her tongue before swallowing. He'd already tasted his, and reveled at the explosion of flavor on his tongue. Rashad scooped more and hummed in fulfillment. "This is amazing."

"It is." India filled her spoon with another portion. "Who knew sour grapes would blend so well with ice cream?" She gasped in fake stun. "Oh wait. Me. Ha." India twirled in place.

Rashad liked that. Although they'd spent quite some time together, she'd never acted so free. He wished she'd spin again. Some hair had fallen from her bun, but India hadn't seen. It looked good hanging loose. Rashad thought it complimented this uncon-fined side of her. She'd normally seem restricted.

Knowing she preferred her hair up, Rashad informed her of the mishap. "Want me to fix it for you?" He asked, resting his cup down.

India hesitated before allowing him to do so. "As long as you know what you're doing."

"I do. Don't worry. I've helped my sister out a few times with things like these." He dried his hands on the towel she carried then went ahead. She kept eating with her back to Rashad. He gladly listened as she rambled on about possible combinations for future flavors. India was on a roll, and Rashad supported it. Her hair sorted, he stepped back. "I think we make a pretty good team," he smiled at her.

Her smile was bright when she returned it. "I think so too."

"I'll call on you to make all my new flavors then. How does that sound?"

"Works for me," India beamed.

Rashad laughed, but inside, a small tendril of hope unfurled.

If he could convince India that they were a good team at this, what else could he show her they'd be good at together?

CHAPTER ELEVEN

"Are you waiting for someone?"

Bright red, blue, and white flags hung on every pole, door, and bench in Sweetgum. The town had veritably transformed in the last few days, becoming a mecca of patriotic coloring in preparation for Memorial Day. Even India's seat had vibrant decorations hanging off the back. She liked seeing folks wearing flags on their bodies. A small one poked out of her front pocket. She'd put on a striking blue blouse with cuffed sleeves and buttons linking its left and right sides. Her top matched with children in similar colors. They ran along Main Street with starry propellers that rotated.

"No, I'm just here to watch," India lied. She looked past the curious woman who'd spoken. An apple bobbing game had been built in front of Rochelle's diner. Mostly men signed up to play. They stood around a short wooden basin of water with arms behind their backs. Many older people gathered to watch while younger kids took interest in other activities. She spotted a carnival game inspired by basketball and noticed how children gravitated towards it. With these added games and snack bars packing the road, it was safe to say that Main Street was unrecognizable. Decorations and carnival games made it difficult for India to find the businesses she'd grown used to.

"Great." The older woman sat beside her. She got something from her purse and held it dearly. "Do you mind helping me light this candle, dear?"

India happily assisted. She took a lighter from the woman's hands and lit the small lamp with red and blue painting. The woman thanked her, then sat in silence. It didn't take long for India to feel out of place. Should she leave? Give this lady some privacy? She might be overthinking this.

He must have gotten too caught up at the shop. She crossed her legs then checked her phone for the time. On days like these, she'd normally explore town with Kim. Last Memorial Day had been great; just them walking and admiring decorations. Malik had joined them later, but India hadn't stuck around after that. She'd left them to venture out together and got back home to finish paperwork. Even having Kim for a short while beat not having her at all.

They'd caught up yesterday on a video call before bed. It seemed Kim was doing good. She and Malik were having a blast touring every park they encountered. India loved listening to Kim's stories so much so that she often forgot to update Kim on her own life. Nothing had changed with India though. She still worked remotely and still missed her best friend. She would have brought up Rashad while they chatted but preferred asking over telling. *Next time*, she thought. If Kim called again, India would mention Rashad. Her best friend deserved to know who she was getting close to. He'd proven to be quite an amazing companion in just a few weeks.

She checked her watch again and sighed. Rashad was a busy guy. Business at his shop must have been hectic. She'd head over there now to check on him. Being in a crowded environment tended to overwhelm her, but Rashad was worth it.

No sooner than she stood did Rashad come bounding. He waved his arm while closing in on her then smiled from ear to ear after stopping. He'd run down the sidewalk to meet her. Sweat dotted his forehead and soaked his collar as heavy breaths left his lungs. He bent forward. "Sorry. Sorry I'm late."

India found his urgency surprising. Had he run the whole way? "It's okay. Take your time with breathing. You look like you're about to pass out." She went to his side to provide support. India touched his back. "Look at you." She felt laughter bubbling inside. "You didn't have to run."

"Of course, I did." He wiped his face with a handkerchief. "We planned to spend Memorial Day together." Despite Rashad's obvious tiredness, his cheer was palpable. "I'm already ten minutes late so let's go ahead and make the most of what little time we have left." Rashad took her hand. "Come on. I heard there's a bottle toss game somewhere around. Someone sent a picture and it looks absolutely exhilarating."

She wouldn't use that word to describe a game so simple but Rashad tended to exaggerate. Her heart hammered as their palms made contact. His hand was so strong and warm. Holding hands reminded her of high school. Back when she'd done so with her crush on a similar outing. She and Rashad weren't dating, but she'd been on a few dates to carnivals like this. A lot of people had. She and Rashad's deep talks over ice cream were quite reminiscent of romantic encounters too. But that wasn't them. They had a strong friendship and that alone. Although... she wouldn't mind—*No.* India refused to entertain this. Not when things were going so smoothly.

They ran past countless games and groups to arrive where Rashad wanted. The two stood in line and observed as a focused man threw colorful rings at glass bottles. The smug attendant folded his arms beside the stand, just waiting for the guy to give in. Meanwhile, spectators encouraged him to press on.

It didn't take long for Rashad to join them. "You can do it. Win a bear. Don't give up now. There's still a chance." Rashad snickered after being outwardly supportive. He nudged India. "I found a trick online on how to win this. You have to toss the ring *over* the bottle.

That's the only way they'll land. If folks here don't make use of that tactic, they'll never win." He shared the attendant's sly smirk.

India liked his confidence. "Look at you doing research for a little game." Rashad sure took goofing off seriously. If that was possible. "Why? Are you scared to lose in front of so many people?" She knew she was. Scrabble wasn't the only game she got competitive over. Being overly competitive was kind of her habit. With every game she played, India became a beast. She just enjoyed excelling at whatever she did. Not a bad trait in and of itself but sometimes, it got out of hand. "I always tell myself no one cares about these things as much as I do. It's how I get through most public contests." She tugged her collar with a nervous laugh.

"Is that how you handled Scrabble?" Rashad shook his head when the guy lost then moved forward. He held India's shoulders to ensure she stayed in front of him. Three people were ahead. The first one already doing warm-ups to try his hands at winning.

"That old thing?" She pretended to act prideful. "I didn't have to." Her shyness returned. "I was having too much fun to think of other people." She heard a chorus of disappointed interjections when the man missed. "I hope your tactic works because I'd hate to embarrass myself." Shivers ran from her waist to her neck. Her palms sweat too. She'd been so down before Rashad got here but now? India could hardly keep still. Was it nerves like she thought or was his energy contagious?

"You won't." Rashad held his hips. "Hey. If you win, which prize will you pick?" He pointed where they hung. Stuffed bears, toy microphones, and other childish playthings were strapped to the back wall. "I think that that big pink bunny would look great in your arms."

India pictured herself dragging the massive toy. "I don't want to carry that with me all night." She pouted at him. "It looks heavy. Plus, we're not five. Why are the prizes so silly? Are these grown men playing to win these for themselves?"

"Some of them might be. But I think most are doing this for their daughters. Or maybe to prove something." Rashad gestured at the man who just lost. He seemed pretty distraught and was now demanding a free retry. But the games didn't work that way. No amount of begging could budge the attendant. "Bottle toss is pretty hard. Every year, people try to beat it but no one is ever victorious."

India had never heard anything more dramatic. "What? But it's just a game." She had to laugh. "I didn't know anyone took it this seriously." She'd see this booth every year but had never been aware of its community or great significance. "What is this? Some sort of rite of passage for men?"

Rashad shrugged as the line moved forward. "For me, it's just fun to beat a con artist at his own game. Look at his smile. He knows his games are rigged."

India would agree that the attendant seemed too pleased at these losses. But to call him a con artist? "Relax. No one in Sweetgum is a con artist. This game is just a little trickier than it looks." She faced Rashad. "And that's what makes it fun."

Her turn finally arrived, and India stepped forward. Quite the crowd had gathered to watch. They each seemed eager to find out who won. So far, not one person had gotten four rings around four bottles. There were twelve in all. They sat in a crate with no spaces between them. India couldn't picture someone drinking from those. They looked toy-like. Each bottle sported a colored cork in its spout. They were glass and shiny, appealing to the eye with their colorful covers.

"Here you are, little Missy." The attendant handed her four rings then hopped back behind the booth.

Rashad clapped for her. "You can do it, India. Win that bunny!" He held out two thumbs, amusing many.

India tittered. Rashad was such a clown. She regained her composure and took aim. Toss them over! India threw her first ring and it landed on a front row bottle. She received cheers which raised her self-esteem. Rashad's over-the-top applause contributed most to her spike in confidence.

"Lucky shot. Let's see you get another." The attendant leaned against his booth's back wall. He snickered when India aimed again. She wasn't sure why this amused him but wouldn't let him discourage her. Everyone else gave serious support. Today, the people deserved to laugh last.

She smiled while throwing the second ring. Another burst of claps and whistles followed. This ring landed on the bottle beside the first. She was off to a good start. This may not have been a competitive sport but its player's attitudes said otherwise. And being who she was, India shared their passion. Mainly for kicks but a lot of her wished for victory as well. "Lucky number three," she mumbled, tossing another like Rashad instructed.

It hit the third bottle rather than landing. The spectators made a unanimous moan of disappointment. That definitely killed India's drive but the support returned instantly. Rashad chanted her name like the goof he was. His behavior not only kept up her morale but the morale of spectators. "Lucky number four!" she called, summoning laughs. She'd stay positive for her sake and the sake of others.

Once again, India missed. She had three rings remaining. Unfortunately, even with Rashad's advice, she could not prevail. Only three bottles were ringed when she ran out of tries. The sorry cheers and 'nice tries' only made the loss more bitter. It was now Rashad's turn and he seemed energized.

"Don't worry. I'll win and get you whatever you want." He winked after whispering close to India's face. She smelled his cologne and felt his tender touch. He'd held her arm to speak. The gesture made goosebumps pop up on her skin, and she shivered, despite the heat of the day. When Rashad finished, she received a soft pat on the head as he snatched his six tries.

She stood aside with some other men as Rashad made a show of aiming. He shut one eye, took on a pitcher's stance then tossed. His theatrics were hilarious. India laughed while folks made endeared comments. An older man asked Rashad if he'd invented tactics to win and the upbeat Rashad happily confirmed. "He's determined to beat this." India added.

Rashad wound up landing his first ring to which she squealed. "Let's go, Rashad," she said with clasped hands. Again, he posed and tossed ridiculously to throw another, and to everyone's delight, it landed! "Now for a third. You can do it." India's hopes skyrocketed. They had to beat this impossible game. She searched for the attendant's reaction and he actually seemed concerned. "Ah-ha!" India loved this. Rashad must have cracked some kind of code. Either that or his strategy was just outrageous enough to work.

Even more people gathered when Rashad ringed another bottle. He began to dance triumphantly as India joined a chant saying 'one more toss'. She clapped and jumped as Rashad prepped himself. When it sailed through the air, she watched with bated breath. If India had a seat, she'd slide off it.

Rashad's ring landed perfectly, and India jumped around, screaming. She couldn't help herself. In all the rejoicing and applause, she ran right to Rashad and threw herself on him; feeling tempted to wrap her legs around his upper half. The man luckily supported her despite her force.

Rashad's chest vibrated as she rubbed her head on it. "Woah there. I know you're excited but don't get too carried away. It's time to choose your prize," he said. Rashad gently removed her then held her wrist to lead her forward. When they stood at the booth counter, he cleared his throat. He seemed to have gained quite the fan club. Loads of older men stood aside to stare, still commending Rashad for his work. He thanked them then held India's arm. "I did it all for her. So, she could have a prize. Told myself that if she didn't win it herself, I'd win it for her." He boasted while the attendant dragged himself forward.

India would admit this was sweet. "Thanks." She rubbed her hands when the bitter worker asked which toy she preferred. "Give me something small and portable."

"Wait what about that?" Rashad pointed out a pink disposable camera. It hung beside the large bunny he'd suggested before. "If you want, we could snap photos of our awesome date. But it's up to you what you choose." He bounced slightly.

India gasped. How hadn't she noticed this amazing option? "Sure. Hand me that camera please." She relished in the attendant's angered glare. Rashad's win was hers too. They took down a tyrant. *That's a bit much.* But being dramatic was fun sometimes.

With their camera, Rashad and India went wild snapping photos. They got snacks at varying stands and took pictures holding them. India once again couldn't resist laughing as they traveled. They played the basketball game, and this time, she won them prizes. But Rashad wouldn't let them stop there. He was determined to try every game. And they probably would have if time hadn't flown so fast. They'd met at sunset but somehow, eight p.m. snuck up on them. Street lights and special memorial lamps in blue and red were lit to illuminate the festival. It showed no signs of slowing down but Rashad did. Which felt out of character since his energy was usually infinite. It wasn't that he'd actually lost steam but more that other obligations awaited him elsewhere.

"But look at all these pictures we took." He chirped while sitting next to India. They'd returned to the bench where everything started. Rashad had laid out every photo they'd taken. He'd stored them in a cross-body bag that came with their first gift. They'd collected several more prizes during their escapade. Some were plushies, others were keychains, and a few had been candy. They'd split them half-half. Right now, India's pockets were stuffed with small chocolate bars. "It'd be a crime if either of us forgot today."

India examined every captured memory. The carnival was just ahead but looked far away. Light shone on them both from the nearby lamp. Below it was a small homemade lamp. Its gentle glow brought on a certain level of tranquility. After such an exciting day, she welcomed its gentle glow. "How could we when we accomplished so much in just a couple of hours?"

"Right." Rashad placed five pictures on India's lap then took five for himself. "Are there any you like more than others?" He faced India with a warm smile.

She contemplated silently. Laughter and running footsteps seemed louder as she did. "This one is really sweet." She picked a photo from Rashad's lap. It featured them making a heart with their fingers. They'd both posed with closed eyes but their joy was unmistakable. "You look so adorable."

"And what about you?" They'd snapped that one after winning at skee-ball. "You were so happy you couldn't keep your eyes open. You're like a puppy getting its chin scratched."

India's heart skipped as he made over her. "Thank you." She tapped the photo. "I like that one best."

"Have it." Rashad placed it with hers. He grabbed another. "I think this one is my favorite." He showed her a picture where they pulled silly faces in line for cotton candy. "I think these poses encapsulate our truest selves. The whacky versions of you and me who deserve to come out more. The parts of us that aren't afraid to have so much fun that we look a little unhinged." He bumped her with his shoulder.

Rashad may not have realized, but his words just now were rather profound. "That's so deep, Rashad." India stacked her tiny pictures together. "I kept feeling this sense of freedom all day. Like I was a kid who didn't care about anything but enjoying myself. You sort of bring that out of me, you know? The unbridled joy of being a care-free child."

"Really?" It was now Rashad's turn to be shy. He scratched the back of his neck. "Wow, India. That's amazing." He checked his watch but seemed unbothered by the time. "I always say that we're our most honest selves at our youngest." He reclined. "And I get to see a glimpse of that whenever I serve ice cream."

He'd said he had to leave at eight. That hour had passed ten minutes ago. India herself always made a point of getting home before dark after going out. Unless she left the house at night, that was. "I do feel younger whenever I eat ice cream. But that goes for all candy."

"Which is why my shop is also a candy place." Rashad seemed pleased with his business decision. "I don't think you've ever tried our candy though. A lot of people forget we're two businesses in one." He gathered his pictures and carefully put them in the pocket of his polo. "The sweetest businesses at that."

India wondered briefly if serving ice cream for a living would brighten her demeanor. *I think Rashad is like this naturally.* Which made her fonder of him. "Next time I stop by, I'll be sure to buy myself some candy along with a scoop."

"Oh please. You're India. You don't have to buy anything. Your first candy order will be free of charge." He patted his pocketed pictures. "Okay, I should get going." He got up. "Today was amazing, but it goes without saying. We always have a great time when we meet up."

A sense of sadness shrouded India. It always came when Rashad said goodbye. They lived separate lives with separate responsibilities. He couldn't stick around forever. India knew this but somehow, parting ways with Rashad caused her deep despair. Like a small child saying goodbye to their companion. She supposed she just enjoyed his company. Maybe a little more than the way a friend liked another. "I had fun today too." She stood. "Thought of any plans for our next adventure?"

Rashad held his hips. "Not yet, but I'm sure something will come to me. Although, if you come to the shop again, we could try making another rare ice cream flavor. What do you say? Chocolate grape swirl?"

India shoved him playfully as he laughed. "You're so crazy." But she loved that about him. "We can experiment with flavors some other time. I swear that between the two of us, I care more about saving your business resources than you do." One day, she wished to acquire half Rashad's nonchalance. Where she worried too much, he didn't at all.

"Relax." Rashad stared down the lighted street. "If creating new flavors for fun was actually harmful, I'd have enough self-control to not do it." He opened his arms. "Goodbye hug?"

She could cry. They'd text later, but it wasn't the same as meeting in person. "Goodbye hug." India squeezed him when her arms held him dearly. She rested her cheek on his chest and let him perch his chin on her head. Her braids were down today. "Safe walk home."

"Same to you. Be careful out there." Rashad glanced at his watch again. "I got some documents to finish up at the shop before I head home. Oh wait. Would it be safer if you tagged along, and I walked you to your place?"

India suddenly felt her phone vibrate. She touched her pocket. Was this Kim? "No, it's okay. Everyone's up and active anyway. Plus, town is pretty safe. You go get your work done. I have a call to respond to." She slid her phone out and grinned as Kim's face lit up on the screen. Just when she'd started feeling down. *Kim to the rescue.*

"Okay cool. But you be careful out there." Rashad waved again then ran off.

India watched him go before answering Kim's video call. "Hi!"

"Hey India. I know we talked yesterday, but I've been missing you. How is everything?" Kim had on a satin cap. A green pillow poked out from her lap and led India to assume she was in bed. The lights in her room were bright, allowing India to see Kim clearly. Apart from seeming a little worn out, her friend appeared to be in good health.

India took a seat, just itching to fill Kim in on Rashad. First, she checked the sidewalk to ensure he'd truly left, then whispered. "I'm so glad you asked because I've been meaning to tell you." She bounced her knees. "As you know, it's Memorial Day, and there's a small carnival here in town."

Kim looked heavily invested already. "Uh-huh?" She rotated her hand to prompt faster storytelling.

Every fun instance with Rashad replayed in India's head. Her heart flipped, and she tried to contain it. "Normally, I go with you, but you know our situation."

"Yes. I really wish I was there."

"Me too, but luckily, I recently made a new friend!" India danced by rocking left and right. "You should know him. His name is Rashad, and he owns the ice cream slash candy shop here in town."

Kim's mouth popped open. "No way. The 'Scoop! There It Is!' guy? The one you said was cute but seemed childish? You and him are together?" Her camera jerked sporadically. India heard squealing as well. When Kim reappeared, her smile was brighter than the sun. "India, that's amazing!"

"Wait no. I never said we were dating. Hold on." India cut Kim's celebration short. The other woman looked lost but attentive. "I said we're *friends*. As in since you've left, we've gotten to know each other and quite enjoy spending time together. It's nothing romantic." She quieted down as a group of boys strolled past her. They had just left the carnival.

"Oh." Kim touched her chin with one finger. "I see." But her face said otherwise. "So, you only see him as a friend and absolutely nothing more?" She leaned closer to the camera, wearing a smirk.

A tingle went down India's spine. As it did, she thought of Rashad. His playful smile and dimples. He had gentle eyes that often switched to mischievous like a fun-loving kid. Today he'd sported a fresh haircut. India hadn't given it much thought, but what if Rashad cut his hair for their date? No. She was getting ahead of herself.

"Aww." Kim gushed on-screen. "Looks like my question made you consider. Do you think you might like him?"

India quickly shook her head. "No. We're really just friends. I'm sure he only sees us as that. And that's how I see him too. It's nice. I'm really glad he reached out after you left. Otherwise, I would've been cooped up in my apartment this evening." She laughed nervously. "I probably wouldn't have left the house since you moved." It was a shame to admit but the truth.

Her reaction also revealed something very important.

Kim was right.

She definitely had feelings for Rashad that went a little beyond friendship.

India wasn't sure when that had changed. She knew that Rashad made her happy, but the realization that she wanted to be more than just his friend hit her like a freight train. How had she done this to herself? Rashad had never said anything about being more than just friends. And here she was, catching feelings for him when he'd been nothing but kind to her.

India had to swallow against the knot in her stomach.

"India?"

Kim's voice snapped her back to reality. "Yeah. Yes. We're definitely just friends."

"Okay. If you say so. It's just interesting to me that he's suddenly taken interest when you and Nate aren't together and I'm not around to steal your attention." Kim shrugged, but India knew what she meant. Her friend was obviously convinced that Rashad had a thing for her.

"I'm flattered that you think there are men waiting for a chance to date me." India cracked up with Kim, who repeated 'they should' through hysterical laughter. As India cooled down, she began to imagine something. What would happen if she and Rashad had another chance to do this night again? What if she told him something that she'd begun to suspect, which was that her feelings for him were a little more than just friends? This time, before he ran off, India would hold his hands and pour out her heart. She would confess to developing feelings with much hesitance but eventually told him everything.

Even in her mental space, Rashad didn't reciprocate her feelings. Awkward silence quickly fell, and the fantasy came crashing down. It shattered like glass, startling her. She had to shake her head to ward off the humiliation. *I really don't want to mess things up.* If she scared off Rashad by confessing, who else would she spend time with? India didn't only see him as a placeholder for Kim but someone special. She'd hate to lose him and would do whatever it took to maintain their friendship. If that meant hiding her budding love, then she'd keep it to herself.

India sighed. If only making friends were easier. Then, loneliness would not follow Rashad's possible rejection. If she had more acquaintances, she'd have companions to choose from if he found it awkward to interact going forward. But no. She'd be completely alone if things ended sourly. At times like these, she really wished she had Nevaeh's boldness. Nevaeh made friends everywhere she went; something India struggled with. She'd ask for advice but already saw it failing. They weren't the same. What worked for her sister would not work for her.

"Everything okay?"

India had once again forgotten about Kim. She smiled sheepishly at her best friend's concern. "Sorry. I can't lie to you Kim." Her shoulders fell. "I *have* developed a tiny crush on Rashad but if I tell him, it'll ruin our friendship," she said with a slight quiver in her voice.

Kim's teasing air dissolved in an instant. "Ah India." She looked away for a second. "My advice would be to confess to prevent complications later, but I understand that you don't want to lose him." She held her chest. "But then again…"

"What?" India noticed Kim's contemplative expression. Her friend's eyes were to the sky as she hummed.

"You never were good at telling when someone liked you." Kim's jovial attitude returned. "So, who knows? He might feel the same way that you do. It's not often that people we see around town decide to befriend us unprovoked. If he wanted nothing more than friendship, he would have reached out earlier, at any point in your lives up to this point. To me, it just seems logical. What do you think?"

India considered Kim's opinion. "You have a point, but I still wouldn't risk it." She rubbed her arm and stared ahead. A group of moms walked by with their children. Each kid had something to say. They held toys and bounced around in elation. Their face-paint made her smile. How pure? Watching them reminded her of Rashad. *Oh boy.* She had to let this go. "Anyway, enough about me. I am just *dying* to hear more about your adventures. What did you guys do today? And don't be shy. I want to hear *every* detail." India crossed her leg and got comfy.

Kim hesitated but started to tell India everything. She listened, or she tried to.

But her mind lingered on Rashad.

What if he did want to be more than friends?

And what if he didn't?

Was she willing to risk losing another friend, all in the name of a romantic connection that may or may not be real?

CHAPTER TWELVE

"It's family day!" Rashad raised Destiny high on Preah's portico, the morning light blessing his niece like the angel she was.

"Family day!" Destiny giggled.

Preah snapped her fingers. "Rashad, pay attention." She stood in the doorway with Destiny's backpack. The sun shone overhead as the wind whistled through the hedges. They bordered Preah's front and back yard in an angular 'U'. As the wind swirled around her ceiling wind chimes, Preah continued. "So, I've packed Destiny's snacks, spare clothes, and favorite toys inside this bag." She held up a princess-themed backpack that didn't fit the aesthetic of her outfit. Preah looked dolled up with well-done hair and makeup that enhanced her features. The woman was fully dressed apart from being barefoot. But other than that, her outfit was complete. It consisted of a matching blouse and skirt.

"I know. You don't need to explain that. I've done this a million times." Rashad put down Destiny and took the bag. The small girl held his leg, pointing at the rattling chimes above. "Yes, Destiny. They sound pretty, don't they?"

Preah smiled at her child then squatted. "Promise to be good with Uncle Rashad today?" She opened her arms.

"Yes!" Destiny skipped into Preah's embrace and planted a kiss on the woman's cheek. In response, Preah kissed her forehead, saying many 'I love you's.

Preah stood again. "Make sure she has a good day so she forgets she's missing Mommy and Daddy. I feel like we're always sending her off with you." She tittered, brushing her nails behind her head.

Rashad placed Destiny's bag on his back. He held the child's hand as she jumped like a rabbit. "That's not true." After thinking back, he changed his mind. "Don't worry. I think introducing children to several guardians is good for them. She not only knows she can trust her parents but her Uncle Rashad too." He'd seen this in a blog post. "Plus, you and Devonte are busy people. I get it. And if you two want to have a date night like now, it's completely understandable. No one's complaining. Not me or little Destiny over here." He hopped with her a couple of times to make her laugh. It worked. She hugged his leg and giggled into his jeans. Nothing pleased Rashad more than seeing her happy. "We're all having fun."

Preah could sometimes be tough, but not even she could resist laughing. Rashad's relationship with Destiny was too wholesome. He knew that for a fact. "You two are adorable." Preah reached in and kissed Rashad's cheek as well. "Now go. I wouldn't want you missing story time at the library." She waved.

"Oh right." He checked his watch then spun around. "Later Pre. And tell Devonte his cologne is awesome. I can smell it from here!" Rashad ran down the short flight of stairs he'd taken to the portico. Destiny saw this as a race and ran past him. She would have gotten far if he didn't have her hand.

His sister barked a long-winded laugh. "I will. Trust me. He'd be happy to know that you like it!"

Rashad watched her wave as he walked backward then faced forward. From there he took Destiny to the sidewalk outside Preah's gate. "Come on D. Let's play airplane to get there." He put her on his shoulders and held her tiny hands. She pretended they were controls, and he moved according to how she used them.

❦

BEING off the clock felt weird. Rashad supervised Destiny, who took pleasure in eating a small cup of ice cream. He'd checked in on his staff while ordering but they'd insisted he didn't have to. As the boss, he only took days off in case of emergencies. Today, since Preah had a date day with Devonte, he'd informed his workers that he'd need one. Being the kind easygoing staff they were, they'd happily made arrangements for this. Michaela had even given him a meaningful look before entertaining Destiny for a couple of minutes. He truly appreciated their understanding but couldn't shake his guilt at not working.

"Oh well." Rashad pushed these thoughts aside to help his niece to scoop her melting dessert. They'd had a ball at the library with other small children. Destiny had even received a new storybook when the reading session ended. The librarian's wife had been today's reader. She'd done an excellent job engaging the kids by using exaggerated voices for the characters. Rashad expected nothing less from a skilled childcare expert. Destiny had had a blast.

"Uncle Rashad, I want a cone," Destiny said with ice cream smeared across her face. She kicked her short legs while pointing to the line.

They sat together in the booth he always shared with India. Sitting here made Rashad kind of miss her, but Destiny had already chosen this spot. He wiped her lips with a napkin. "When you get big, you can have one, but for now, we'll stick to cups."

Destiny watched enviously as seated patrons licked cones of varying colors and sizes. "Mommy says I can have the cone. Mommy and Daddy. They said that." Her bright eyes looked mischievously at Rashad. "And they said..." Destiny paused in thought, thoroughly amusing Rashad. He'd let her know not to lie when she finished. "They said that your girlfriend said I can have a cone too." She smiled, and her little white teeth twinkled.

"Girlfriend?" Rashad's heart jumped, but Destiny didn't notice. She kept giggling. If there was one thing he'd learned from babysitting all these years it was that children's perception knew no bounds. "Mommy and Daddy think I have a girlfriend?" He'd brought up India on one or two occasions but never mentioned his feelings. Did Preah pick up on them? Rashad felt exposed.

Destiny took her spoon from his hand. "They said that Uncle Rashad will have a girlfriend and Uncle Hakim will be the one that's always alone because Uncle Rashad had a girlfriend." The child took a spoonful of ice cream and chucked it in her mouth. Her words were still so small... she said "Uncle" in a way that sounded like "Unca," and while it made Rashad's heart squeeze, the message underneath made him want to sigh with frustration.

His sister was such a busybody.

Rashad would act surprised that they talked about him behind his back, but he knew better than to expect anything else. As Preah's brother, it was inevitable that she'd discuss him with her spouse. He just wished that whenever she talked about him or Hakim, it didn't sound so... dismissive. Pre-determined. He was his own person, and he didn't want his sister thinking he was so predictable.

"That's cute D, but I don't have a girlfriend. And if I did, she wouldn't say you can have a cone." He pushed his nose against hers, making Destiny laugh. "And I *know* Mommy and Daddy didn't say you could have a cone either. Don't lie Destiny. Uncle will always know when you're lying." He pulled back and seized the spoon. "Plus, lying is very bad. Don't be like the boy who cried wolf. He lied so much that no one ever believed him again. Even when he told the truth."

Destiny gasped. "Wolf?" She seemed frightened. "I don't want a wolf to eat me. I'm sorry."

"Good girl." Rashad kissed her forehead then let her eat by herself. He put his arm on the backrest then sighed. To call India his girl. What a privilege that would be. Too bad she wasn't ready. Or at least he thought she wasn't. *I need advice.* And since Preah was already interested, she may be the right person to seek it from.

THERE'D BEEN a face painter at the park this afternoon. In true preschooler fashion, Destiny had begged and cried for face painting, but Rashad hadn't let her. Normally, he'd oblige to her every whim but not today. By the time they'd arrived, it was already late. It seemed redundant to get her face painted when they'd be heading home soon.

As a result, she'd thrown a tantrum. Even now, the child just would not talk to him or anyone else. Preah had sent Devonte upstairs to cheer her up thirty minutes ago, but the father still hadn't returned. After he'd left, Preah had offered Rashad some tea, so the two currently held mugs in the kitchen.

Rashad sat at the table, watching steam float from his cup. "I should have just given her what she wanted." As far as he could hear, Destiny wasn't screaming, but that didn't mean the crying had stopped.

Preah blew on her cup. "No, you did the right thing. If you hadn't, I'd be cleaning face paint off of a bawling Destiny as we speak." She hadn't changed her outfit. Preah still looked fabulous, but this time she had heels to complete her fancy look. When Rashad had gotten back, he'd caught her and Devonte unlocking the front door. Preah tended to call early when it came to bringing Destiny home. "I'm glad you put your foot down." She winked.

"Thanks." But he wasn't one for strictness. Saying no had been hard. "Anyway." He faced the over-sink window, noting the neighborhood lights brightening the streets. "I wanted to talk to you about something."

His sister put down her mug. "Is it serious? You hardly ever sound serious, but you do now. What's going on?" She knitted her brows in evident concern.

Rashad had trouble gathering his thoughts. He sat back as Preah waited. "I wouldn't say it's as serious as something like changing careers or health issues." He observed how the kitchen lights reflected in his cup. The man took careful sips that warmed his belly. "But it is important." He brushed his fingertips against his neck. "I wanted to know your thoughts on India and how I should move forward with her." He worked up the nerve to meet Preah's eyes again.

"Oh." At first, she seemed stunned, but it didn't last. "So, you admit it then?" Preah sipped her tea.

He detected slickness in her face and intonation. "Yes. I'd admitted to *myself* a long time ago that I like her, but it seems you decided she was my girlfriend way before that." There, he brought it up. "Don't act all surprised. I heard Destiny this afternoon. You and Devonte call India my girl." He raised an accusatory finger.

"What?" Preah faked shock before laughing. "Okay, I won't pretend. You caught me. It's just the way you talk about her whenever she comes up." She proceeded to perform a stunning Rashad impression. "Oh, I wasn't at the shop that day. I was out with *India*. Preah, India's so good at Scrabble. Sorry Pre, but I have something with India later. Can we reschedule family game night?"

"Hey, the last part didn't happen. I'd never reschedule family game night," he said in defense of himself.

Underneath his sister's attitude, though, he could tell that she was hurt. Watching her made Rashad embarrassed. He picked up his mug again. "But you are right about my feelings." From morning to night, India ran through his mind. Even now, he couldn't resist wondering where she was, what she did, and her thoughts. It was maddening. "No one's ever complimented me like India does. Our personalities just work." He smiled at his beverage. "She's tame. It keeps me mellow. Except when she gets competitive. Then I'm the mellow one." Playing bottle toss with her had become a core memory. "We both like games and ice cream. She listens to me, I *love* listening to her, and we just work. Man, I love India so— I mean." He lost it just now, and his brain fogged up.

"Aww," Preah caught on to what he was saying so fast, his mind whirled. "Rashad, are you saying what I think you're saying?"

Rashad didn't get the chance to let his mind catch up. "Um. I… Well…"

Preah went to town with it; teasing and grinning. "Rashad, that's amazing. You think you love her?" Her face softened in adoration.

He'd never gotten nervous in Preah's company until now. "I… I'll say I think she's the one." His palms were sweating. They wet the outside of his mug. Rashad blew on its contents as his sister went berserk. She couldn't keep still and said many congrats. "But I don't want to scare her. Her best friend just left her alone in town, and she's really reserved so that's why I've been holding back."

Preah put her mug aside to hold her cheeks. "Do you think she likes you back?"

Rashad remembered when she hugged him on Memorial Day. Even their goodbye hug had left something lingering. A message from India's heart to his. "I think so."

Preah smacked her hands together, the clap resonating with finality. "Well perfect. It sounds like you guys will have quite the happy life together." Preah spoke with confidence. "But I get what you mean by not wanting to scare her." She held up her hands as if halting him. "So, if I were you, I'd wait for the right time. You two seem to have a connection. Use that connection to read her; to feel when the time is perfect to open up."

She seemed so sure. It put Rashad at ease. He'd drawn that conclusion before, but hearing Preah echo his words assured him that he was on track. "Okay. Thanks, Preah. I'll do that."

She seemed so sure. It put Rashad at ease. He'd drawn that conclusion before, but hearing Preah echo his words assured him that he was on track. "Okay. Thanks, Preah. I'll do that."

She smiled reassuringly. "I'm happy for you. You deserve love. I haven't met India yet, but she sounds really special. Cherish her."

"Believe me, I will." Rushed footsteps came down the staircase, grabbing their attention. As Rashad and Preah peeped through the kitchen doorway, they frowned. "Devonte?" said Rashad.

Preah's husband seemed out of sorts. His tie was gone, and his blazer was missing. The man had sweat stains on his dress shirt. "It's done. I finally put her down. She was calm for the most part, but it took a lot of effort to get her that way." He dragged himself in and sat beside Rashad. "Kids are really something else."

Preah and Rashad locked eyes then laughed heartily. Devonte closed his eyes and shook his head while his wife got up to pour him some tea.

Rashad relaxed, soaking in the familiar companionship with his sister and brother-in-law. In the back of his mind, he worried over what to do about India. He knew how he felt.

But would she feel the same?

CHAPTER THIRTEEN

India tossed her grocery bags on the counter before pacing back and forth. She went over and over what she needed to do, but she couldn't bring herself to do it.

She didn't want to lose Rashad as a friend by telling him she had feelings for him. Especially if those feelings weren't reciprocated.

And, given what she'd just seen, she thought maybe he was hiding some secrets of his own.

"Rashad," India sighed. She grabbed the back of her head. As India stopped by the sink, she got lost staring outside. Remnants of sunlight lingered in clouds as the sun gradually sank. Sunsets had a knack for calming her down, but today's setting sun didn't have that effect.

India gave her back to the window and stared in space. "We've known each other for weeks," she said to her empty apartment.

How could he hide from her that he had a child?

Part of her thought that he wouldn't. Rashad wouldn't keep something so vital a secret. In the time they'd spent getting acquainted, she'd learned plenty. Rashad's hobbies, dislikes, and preferences were all stored in her mind. She supposed they hadn't dived much into family life, but being a dad wasn't easy to hide.

She'd imagine that being a single dad was even harder to keep secret. Rashad had been clear on his relationship status. He had no significant other. That meant he had to be raising the child alone.

Saturdays were Sweetgum's designated shopping days. From morning to evening would find residents crisscrossing through town with lists and shopping bags. India usually gave her best effort to head out early and come back before noon, but today she'd had some work to attend to that set her back. She'd ended up leaving her home at ten a.m. instead of eight and as a result, had gotten back at three.

It was on her way home that she'd walked past Sweetgum Park, happening to see Rashad there too. India had wanted to wave and catch up but had stiffened at the sight. A child no older than four had been with her friend, crying as he struggled to appease her. She'd hidden behind a food truck outside to not be spotted.

India wasn't one for snooping but could not resist. Questions upon questions had piled in her brain as she wondered who this kid could be and why Rashad seemed so close to her. They even looked alike to India. She prided herself on being mature and using communication rather than making assumptions but the shock had been too much. Instead of approaching and asking, she'd hurried home in the opposite direction. What started as brisk steps had turned to full-on leaps as she high-tailed it out of there.

She presently unpacked her groceries, giving it more thought. He was always at the shop. Not *once* did a child ever come up when they spoke. Even if he was a part-time dad, she knew in her heart that he would be all in. Rashad wouldn't see his own kid as an afterthought. No way. Which was probably why he'd been spending the afternoon with her. It could have been mandatory but a dedicated father would never neglect to mention his kid. "Exactly. He's sweet." She'd always pictured him being a fun dad. A man involved with his kids in every aspect. School, playtime, sports, and all else. If he *did* have children, he would have mentioned them. As for why she'd already given thought to Rashad in a parenting role? India's mind sometimes wandered. And when it did, he was what she thought of. It was hard being away from him after spending all day together.

India just put two milk cartons in the fridge. She closed it and stared at her magnets. This exact scenario had happened to Nevaeh. Where she'd assumed Tia was Sean's daughter since they were close. Something similar might be the case with Rashad. That little girl didn't have to be his. "And if she is?"

The conflicted woman sat at her table. Darkness was beginning to swallow her apartment. She wanted to switch the lights on but felt too tormented. She'd never judge Rashad for having children nor would she stop spending time with him, but India just wasn't sure about filling a parenting role for a child. Apart from that, she wouldn't mind dating a single dad. "I'm jumping to conclusions."

She put her elbows on the table, now rubbing her forehead. Rashad had never voiced any form of romantic attraction to her but hypothetically, India wouldn't lose interest over this. Would she?

Being raised by a single mom gave her an appreciation for single parents. He may have had a partner in the child's mother but India wasn't sure. If Rashad had a business *plus* a kid looking after, he must have been incredible. Only the strongest could juggle so many responsibilities. She admired him more for facing both roles head on but was hurt he'd never told her. "It probably isn't my business." She mumbled, slipping out her phone. She needed an outside perspective. She knew Kim was scheduled to explore the Andes today but India required urgent advice. Even if Kim was incapable of replying instantly, India would have at least vented.

She hit record in their chat and unloaded what weighed on her chest. Her fears, doubts, and concerns poured out. She'd turned on the lights while walking back and forth, changing from one spot to the next. When all was said and done, India was on the counter. She hadn't realized how much she'd moved but changing places helped with thinking.

"Did I really rant for two minutes?" The voice note showed how long she'd spoken. Hopefully, Kim wouldn't mind. Her friend often encouraged her to speak since India tended to bottle her emotions. She just hoped Kim would find the time to listen. With everything going on with her, Kim had less of that each day. India would hate to waste it with petty rambling. Her line of thinking was toxic but hard to shake. She'd just never been in such a dilemma. Would Kim find her annoying? Too whiny?

India was just contemplating hitting 'delete' when her phone rang. She jolted then read the ID. "Kim?" So soon?

She hit 'answer' with a shaking leg, watching her feet hover above the floor.

"India oh my God," Kim said urgently. "I just listened to your voice note. You sound terrified!"

India hopped off the counter in restlessness. From there, she went back to pacing. "Aren't you supposed to be hiking? How did you respond so fast?" She crossed her free arm while strutting to the sink.

"Our activities today were canceled. It's raining cats and dogs where I am but let's unpack this. You saw Rashad with a kid at the park today?" India heard faint rainfall on the other end. There was also the shifting of sheets as if Kim had risen from lying down.

India leaned back on the sink, chewing her bottom lip. "Yes. It was this little girl. She was so adorable but they were alone. I don't know. The way he handled her just screamed 'dad'. Like he'd dealt with this child before, and he was really comfortable with her." She combed fingers through her hair then chewed her inner lip.

Kim went quiet for a second. "Okay but it's not like he confirmed she was his. You just saw something." She said some words incoherently then spoke up again. "Didn't this exact same scenario happen to your sister? What's with the two of you and single-daddy issues?"

"It's not impossible for him to be her dad." India faced the window a second time. It was dark out with no traces of light left. "With

Nevaeh, she didn't stick around when Tia ran in. She just stormed out but I stayed and watched. You know I'm good at reading people. He just seemed really fatherly with that child." Her heart would not stop racing. "We've talked about everything under the sun, but somehow, he forgot to mention he's a father. Do you think he didn't to not scare me off? Or maybe he's like my dad and is only partially part of his child's life." She found herself back at the table, sitting sideways on her seat. "But he doesn't seem like that kind of man. To only commit halfway to such an important role." Just then, glimpses of her past hit her like a wave. She and Nevaeh would spend a lot of time at Kim's place but saw their dad every other weekend. He wasn't the worst dad, but not the best either. But that could just be her experience.

"Okay India; breathe. I think you're letting your own feelings twist your sense of logic," Kim said evenly. She directed a brief breathing exercise which India followed. Kim sometimes did that when India over-thought. It was at times like these that she appreciated her. Someone who understood her needs and met them. "I do think that your people reading skills are unmatched, but we need to pace ourselves. You know Rashad better than I do. Would he really not mention his daughter if he had one?"

India had gone over this with herself. She dragged her chair towards the table and rested her free arm on it. "Probably not, but people can keep secrets." She scratched her cheek self-consciously, finding interest in the burl of her wooden table. "And we haven't even known each other a year yet. It's not completely impossible."

Kim sighed. "Look, you should learn from your sister's mistake. Most times, things aren't what they seem. You like Rashad, but you're too scared to tell him. For all we know, this could be you subconsciously finding reasons to not confess. I know you, India. You do that sometimes."

India sat taller with a twisted mouth. She picked at the edge of her table nervously. "I do not." She knew Kim wasn't lying, but she didn't want to confront Rashad either. "Okay, I do, but that's not what's happening here. I just feel hurt and a little betrayed, even though I shouldn't. I'm sorry. I must sound like I'm whining over nothing." An unwilling laugh burst out of her, but she forced herself to stop when Kim responded.

"No, you don't. Your worries are valid. Plus, I love catching up with you. Even if it's just to give some advice."

That touched India's heart. "You're so sweet."

"It's just me being the best friend I can. You've done tons of great things for me too. Most way more thoughtful than what I'm doing." Kim paused as if reminiscing then exhaled shortly. "Anyway, don't write Rashad off yet. I get the feeling this is just another misunderstanding. We also have evidence that it is. He never mentioned a daughter when you talked, he doesn't seem like the kind of guy who'd be neglectful to his kid, and I think we would have heard of the ice cream man's daughter. He's popular."

India wasn't sure about that last part. "Sweetgum isn't the biggest town, but it's not small enough to know specific details on everyone's lives. Especially not someone we don't know personally." She scanned her kitchen to rid herself of anxious thoughts. Distractions were proven to ease anxiety. "But everything else you've said is spot on."

"Great. If you want, you can bring it up the next time you two meet."

"Yes. I should." But she probably wouldn't for fear of embarrassment. Normal people didn't spy on their friends. "Anyway, thanks for the chat, Kim. We'll catch up later."

"Sure. Take it easy." Kim hung up after saying goodbye.

CHAPTER FOURTEEN

Rashad made sure to get home early after closing today. After wiping down every counter, he'd rushed to the exit while thinking of India. They had a Scrabble date at her place that he wasn't going to miss.

"And what about the troublesome back lock?" Joel asked through Rashad's truck window. The man was on the sidewalk. A few street lights had already come on. It was after six-thirty but the sun hadn't fully set. That was just summer; long days.

Rashad buckled his seatbelt as the engine heated up. "Just pull the door in while you lock it. I figured out a hack this morning." He informed with hands on the wheel. Rashad stuck his head out after putting his truck in 'drive'. "Now if you'll excuse me, I have some-where to be by eight." He saluted a laughing Joel and drove out of his parking spot.

"You go tiger," said Joel.

Rashad cruised out of the parking lot excitedly. He'd given Preah's advice some long hard thought and decided to trust his gut. India still wasn't ready to know his true feelings. It hurt that he'd have to hide them until she was but as long as they spent time together, Rashad would not mind. He just wished he hadn't fallen so hard already. Just over the weekend he'd grown more infatuated. He'd asked himself again and again if this was normal. The answer wasn't clear but he liked being smitten. It brought him a certain level of joy that couldn't be replicated. Unless maybe India decided to date him.

His phone rang as he drove down Main Street. For a second, he thought it might be India, calling to cancel. His heart sank at the very notion but Rashad gathered his wits. After reading 'Pops' as the ID he calmed down.

"Hey Dad. How you doing?" Rashad took a corner and drove smoothly from there.

"Hey son. I'm doing really good," the older man replied. "Listen, remember when I said Betsy looked ready to give birth any time between this week and next?"

Rashad was puzzled. "Betsy?" His dad made sure to keep him posted on every development on the farm. Doing so was essential since Rashad was its top client. Rashad knew every cow's name and their schedule. He also worked there from time to time with his dad but that was mainly on weekends. Preah and Hakim would lend a helping hand too. In fact, if Rashad wasn't mistaken, they should be there now. Preah liked the exercise that came with farm life while Hakim was needed for muscle. The same went for Devonte. And since her parents often visited, little Destiny had grown used to staying there as well. He bet right now she was having a ball chasing goats. "Her last trimester went by already?" He counted in his mind. Rashad always tried to stick a pin in relayed information from the farm but sometimes fell short. His hectic life and business were to blame for these lapses in memory. "Oh yes! She should have been due this week. How could I forget something like that?" India deserved some blame too. For consuming his head space when Rashad tried to focus.

His old man laughed. "Don't sound guilty for forgetting. Happens to the best of us." Rashad heard his boots crunching hay. There were soft conversations in the background as well. He recognized his mother's voice. "Anyway, you know the tradition. We all need to be there for our animals. Betsy's doing well already but I'm sure she'd do even better if you stopped by. It also wouldn't hurt to lend a hand if you can. You just got off work at the shop, right?"

Rashad clenched his teeth as he entered the street he lived on. He slowed down and parked beside someone's lawn. "Yes. I did. I made plans but looks like I'll have to cancel them. Tell Betsy to hang in there. I'm not missing this." Though it did pain him to cancel on India. He'd been starved of her all weekend. "Unless…" A light bulb dinged over his head.

"Unless what?"

Rashad forgot his dad on the line. "Sorry. Was talking to myself but would it be okay if I brought a friend with me?"

"Of course! The more the merrier."

Rashad loved his dad's easygoing character. "Great. Later Dad." He hung up then dialed India.

"Hey Rashad." She sounded a little flat, not at all like her usual self. Rashad's mind tripped over her tone, but then she seemed to brighten up in the next sentence. "Ready to get absolutely annihilated by my word skills?"

He smiled at her question. "Look who's getting cocky?" Rashad breathed out. "Honestly, I was completely ready to cream you in all ways conceivable but a cow on my dad's farm's giving birth and I need to be there to oversee the process." He sensed her deflation. "But don't worry. We don't have to cancel. We probably won't be playing Scrabble this evening but we could witness the beauty of birth." Rashad winced once the words left his mouth. He should have phrased it differently. What if birth disgusted her? He may have loved supervising such things due to his upbringing, but India wasn't like him. "Or we could just reschedule for tomorrow."

India gasped. "Oh my gosh, I'd be honored. Baby animals are so adorable. Thank you so much for inviting me to come, Rashad. I'm changing right now. Can you pick me up?"

What an amazing woman. He wouldn't have judged if she'd

denied his request, but her interest delighted him. Could she be any more perfect? He had a brief vision of them rearing goats together. She wore denim overalls and a straw hat in his fantasy. Farm girl India was something he didn't know he needed. "Yes. I'm coming. And it was my pleasure to invite you." He hung up and drove out of his parking spot. India kept giving him reasons to love her.

THEY'D DRIVEN past the hiking trails to get here. His dad's farm was as typical as it got in terms of farm grounds. An unpainted picket fence lined the dirt road to get there, and plenty of fields for grazing spanned the territory. The barn house was a red and white structure serving as the farm's central point. At daytime, cows and goats grazed outside before settling inside it to rest. There was a petting zoo to its left with a plastic banner and arrows giving directions to where this zoo was located. Inside were posts for goats, horses, and bunnies. Each animal had a designated section blocked off by hay stacks and gates. The zoo had become quite the attraction since its inception but was currently closed.

Rashad ran with India to the barn, making out a raking Hakim outside. The large man wore garden gloves as he worked.

"You're a little late. She just gave birth five minutes ago." Hakim dusted dirt off his hands. He noticed India and greeted her stiffly.

"Aw man." Rashad scratched his head. "We can at least take a look at the calf. What do you say, India?" Before the words left his mouth, she hurried in, seeming eager for a glimpse. "Wait for me." He followed her and was now inside.

They walked on stray hay until reaching Betsy's stall. It wasn't hard to find. All India had to do was follow the sound of voices. No other stall had people in them.

Rashad greeted the other cows and horses, then stopped beside India in the doorway. "Would you look at that?" His soul soothed at what he met.

Betsy lay on her side with Preah next to her. The vet was standing with a plastered grin while Rashad's parents snapped photos. Next to Betsy's belly were two brown calves. They seemed kind of damp, but their soft towels dried the excess water.

"Hi everyone." India said a greeting before stepping in. She did so carefully after whispering, seeming completely enthralled by the sight. When she was close enough, she covered her mouth. "This is amazing. Oh my gosh." Sparkling tears sat in her eyelids. They looked like crystals under the light. Each stall had one light bulb on the back wall. It seemed each one had been turned on for Betsy's delivery. "Your cow and calves are beautiful." India faced Rashad's parents.

His mom put her phone away with a laugh. "Thank you, sweetie. This your first time seeing something fresh out of the womb?" Her phrasing got a laugh from his dad and Preah.

Rashad found himself chortling too. India seemed so captivated. "I'm sure she's seen babies or at least puppies. Never had a dog who gave birth to puppies, India?" It suddenly clicked that this was India's first time meeting his family. This was usually a big deal for couples, but they weren't dating, so he'd relax. India didn't look intimidated at all.

Preah rolled her eyes on the ground. "Why would she? That's not common. We've had the experience because we raise animals. Most folks don't, so don't worry about it India," Preah smiled. She got up and dusted her pants. Everyone but Rashad and India looked dressed for hard work. Gloves encased Preah's hands, and she wore large boots. India had put on a flannel and jeans, but her sneakers didn't fit the setting. Rashad, on the other hand, looked most out of place in his parlor uniform.

"There's a dog here too?" India seemed keen on finding it.

His dad puffed out his chest. "Yup. Livestock guardian dog. Got two of them just in case. The first two are retired. They stay in the house with me and Sherril." He gestured to his wife. "We've had a lot of animals come and go since starting this little farm." His teeth bared in a full smile as he looked down at Betsy. Her calves suckled on her breast milk. They seemed at peace beside her as she watched them feed. "And it looks like a brand-new generation is coming in right before our eyes."

India nodded then wiped her eyes. "The miracle of life." She backed up until beside Rashad again.

Rashad fought the urge to put his arm around her. "Yes. The miracle of life." She looked so content and peaceful. "So, you're an animal lover?"

India seemed bashful. "I wouldn't say that since I've never had any pets. I'm more of an animal secret admirer." His parents laughed, and she rubbed her hands. "I don't think I'll ever have the guts to hold or pet one. But I love watching them from afar."

"Is that so?" Their vet's name was Dr. Brown. He'd been tending to their pets and farm animals since Rashad could remember. By now he'd grown a grey beard and had lost all his hair. Rashad recalled a time where he'd been fit. Now, his belly protruded from every shirt he wore. "We can change that. I think you're more than ready to reach out and touch the critters you admire." He pulled his arm off the wall and stepped up to India. "That little one's all done feeding. She even looks ready to walk. I bet she'd love it if you gave her a pat on the head."

India's eyes widened. "A pat on the head? Um... well..." She played with her fingers to the endearment of everyone.

"You can do it, India. There's nothing to be scared of." Rashad went ahead and cheered her on. His parents and sister did the same, coaxing her gently. He was just about to pull his phone out for a picture when someone behind him tapped his shoulder.

It was Hakim, and he seemed tired. "Come help me clean up some grass that Dad cut earlier. It's not much. Just a small pile next to the barn. Devonte and Destiny are there too."

Rashad wanted to see India face her fears, but his brother needed him. "I'll be right back." He left when India stooped beside the baby animals. She seemed nervous, but Preah continued encouraging her. He couldn't imagine a more perfect sight.

OUTSIDE, Rashad carried a shovel full of weeds to a wheelbarrow. His brother had failed to mention the four other piles of grass that he'd raked. Devonte placed them in an iron dustpan with Destiny by his leg. Rashad worked close to them, using the single light outside to see.

"Thanks so much for your help, guys." Hakim leaned on the barn wall and drank some water. "You're a great team."

Devonte wiped his forehead with the sleeve of his flannel. "We're not football players." He patted Destiny's head to keep her in check. She'd started bouncing against him. "I saw you coming in here with someone," he said to Rashad. "Is that the girl?"

Rashad could already hear their teasing. "Yes. India wanted to see, so I let her tag along. She's inside with Preah, probably playing with the calves right now." The thought made him gush. "She's not as used to animals as we are, so she was scared to hold one when I left. But I'm sure she's conquered those fears. She's a fighter, that one." He had to stop himself from going on. It wasn't often they asked about India, but when they did, he tended to ramble.

Hakim held down his water bottle. "I'm sure she is." They heard soft footsteps on the weeds and looked forward. "Oh. Speak of the devil." He used his lips to gesture to India skipping in.

Rashad got flustered when she ran up to him with a waving hand. "Oh hey." He sensed his own face light up as she stopped in front of him. "Someone looks excited." Devonte and Hakim's snickers didn't matter. Rashad wasn't ashamed of expressing his devotion. He was but a small ring on India's finger, completely wrapped around it.

"I am because I did it! I pet the calves!" She showed Rashad her hand, which revealed no indication of this.

He celebrated with her regardless. "I am so proud of you! See? Animals are our friends. Wasn't it soothing? I know that whenever I pet my parents' dogs, I feel rejuvenated. Did petting the calves have that effect on you?" Rashad was enjoying every second of India's joy. She was like a child who'd gotten a puppy for Christmas.

India opened her hand to her face. "I think so. They were so cute and sweet." She looked from Devonte to Hakim and said a soft greeting. Her gaze went to Destiny last. For some reason, she fell silent.

Rashad sensed her concernment. Should he formally introduce India to his family? That may break the ice for her. He'd picked up that India disliked unfamiliarity, especially in people. "This is my—"

"Uncle Rashad, look!" Destiny interrupted him by running to his leg. She held a pile of grass in her arms which Devonte disapproved of. Despite her father's demands to bring it back, she threw them on Rashad's body. Now the little girl laughed and hopped around. "Surprise!"

Devonte marched forward to snatch her arm. "Destiny, Daddy just piled that together. Look what you did. Now I have more work to do. That's not fair. You're being naughty," he wagged a stern finger at his daughter.

Destiny looked a little sorry, but since she was still a toddler, she mostly was apologizing to comply with her father's wishes. She asked for Rashad's rake to clean up, but he didn't let her. This seemed to upset Destiny, but Rashad was gentle. He stooped to explain why it was best that she left the cleaning to them.

All the while, India watched in shock and awe. If Rashad didn't know any better, he'd say she was embarrassed. As for why? He didn't know. Though curious, he refrained from asking in front of his family. Rashad would prefer to not put her on the spot.

CHAPTER FIFTEEN

ncle Rashad. India twiddled her thumbs on the way home. Anyone else would put two and two together. Every bit of evidence should have made it abundantly clear that Rashad had no children. He'd never mentioned any, and she'd never seen him with a child besides on Saturday. However, she had known he had a sister. He'd spoken of her before. She even recalled seeing a 'congratulations' flier in the parlor's window for his sister's newborn a few years ago. Back then, India hadn't given it a second thought, but after finding Rashad handling a child, this should have come back to her. But alas, it hadn't until said child called him 'uncle'.

She felt silly. Of course Rashad didn't have a child... he was a great uncle.

And India had jumped to conclusions, all so she wouldn't have to face how she felt about him.

Rashad sailed down Main Street, whistling a song. He'd been doing so since they settled in his truck. They'd spent time gushing over calves but not for long. India just couldn't forget what she'd heard. It should have come as a relief but her shame was too much.

Had she really almost let an assumption drive a wedge between them? She'd been ready to write off Rashad just yesterday. Her justification being she wasn't sure about having children. Not yet anyway. It was something she had to think about, and Rashad possibly having a child of his own had scared her. She'd hate to be an uncertain parental figure in Rashad's kid's life. There were also her fears that Rashad was like her father. India shouldn't have judged or jumped to conclusions, but Kim was right. Her past experience had made her cautious. Overcautious even. So overcautious that she'd nearly let it prevent her from exploring what they had. For now, it was nothing but she badly wanted more. To know him as a lover and cherish their relationship. If only she knew for sure that he shared her feelings. This uncertainty was her source of hesitation.

"Alright. Home sweet home." Rashad parked outside the apartment building. "It's pretty dark, so make sure you go inside quickly. Just in case."

India appreciated his concern. "You do this all the time." She unbuckled her seatbelt and popped the door open. "No one is out to get me in Sweetgum. I'll be fine. Plus, it's a short walk away, and there are too many witnesses." She was referring to a mother and daughter entering the lobby. Other passersby traveled along the sidewalk.

"I know, but it's just a habit. I do this with everyone I care deeply about." He shrugged shyly, looking at his hand on the wheel. Rashad seemed nervous all of a sudden. Scared to make eye-contact.

India liked his shy side. She also loved what he'd admitted. "I care about you too."

He looked at her, and they stared in silence for five whole seconds.

"I should get going." She swung her leg outside the door and hopped out. It was only after shutting it behind her that an idea came to mind. She turned around and pushed her head through the window. "Would you like to come in?"

"I LIKE HOW ORGANIZED EVERYTHING IS," Rashad admired her living room after a brief house tour. She'd shown him every room and where she stored food. Right now, she was in the kitchen getting some snacks while he examined her DVD collection. He'd asked for permission to have a look while she worked.

India waltzed in with a tray of drinks and sandwiches. She found Rashad squatting in front of her TV stand. He held a red DVD case in front of him. "I know DVDs are kind of obsolete these days, but I've invested way too much to just toss them aside. Instead, I figured I'd organize and display them. I like order when it comes to my things. Makes them easier to find." She put the food down on the center table. "That's why my DVDs are color-coded. When I do my spring cleaning, I switch it up." She went to his side and squatted next to him. Somehow, having him here felt right. Like he belonged in her space. She could get used to this. *Very* used to having him over. "For a full six months, I'd had these organized by year of release, and for another, I organized them alphabetically."

His eyes popped in amazement. "That's impressive. I wish I could arrange my stuff that well." He laughed. "But I never have the discipline to keep them that way." He put back the Christmas movie. "I think I like this arrangement because the color coding just satisfies me in ways I can't describe." He moved his finger along the spine of each movie. They started with dark colors on the left shelf then got lighter on the right. India's stereo sat between both shelves of movies. "It's like a color-coded rainbow."

She giggled then stood. "I made some sandwiches. Let's eat them on the couch." India extended a hand to help Rashad to his feet.

Rashad gladly accepted it and got up.

They were sitting comfortably seconds later. Rashad had eaten four cheese sandwiches already. She'd luckily made a bunch, bearing in mind how hard he'd worked today. Between running his business within working hours and helping on the farm at night, he must have been exhausted. She'd assisted with some yard work and was famished herself. These sandwiches were as much for her as they were for him.

"Mm," said Rashad in satisfaction. He reached for another triangle of cheese and bread. "You were pretty fast in there when you made these. It only took you fifteen minutes."

India finished her second one. "I'll confess that I made a good portion earlier for our Scrabble date. I slapped a few extras together since we'd been on the farm so long." She melted at the memories. "That calf was so adorable. Its sweet breaths and heartbeat are something I'll never forget. How many calf births have you seen? You guys seem so accustomed in terms of baby animals. Oh, it was the best experience to watch them cuddle close to their mother and see the world for the first time. I could just…" It suddenly dawned on her that she was rambling. She stopped as Rashad smiled. "Sorry. I got carried away. It's all just new for someone like me."

Rashad took yet another sandwich. There were ten left. India hoped he'd wash it down with her homemade lemonade. She'd prepared it on Sunday to have with daily meals. "I don't know why you're apologizing. I'd listen even if you talked about rocks. I just love hearing you talk." He seemed lost in her face. "I mean…" The man scratched his head. "What I mean is that it's just amazing when people openly express themselves. I think we're at our bests when we speak freely about what we love. So never stop yourself from 'babbling' because it's technically not that if you enjoy what you're saying."

India tapped him fondly. "It is if I keep repeating the same thing with no direction. But I understand what you mean, and I'm glad you said it. You seem so full of wisdom sometimes. Does ice cream make people wiser?" she asked jokingly.

Rashad shrugged. "Who knows? It needs to be researched." He shared her humorous air. "But seriously, I love hearing you talk. It's one of my favorite parts of our friendship." The man chucked another sandwich into his mouth. It didn't take long for him to gobble it up. Now, he lifted the short glass of lemonade she'd poured him. "I get the feeling not a lot of people here in Sweetgum get to listen to you. Am I correct?"

Just a few weeks ago, she'd been complaining about loneliness. Aside from the general interactions that came with grocery shopping and running other errands, India didn't really chat with others. At least not at length. Now and then she talked to Nevaeh but that was infrequent. "You're right. I'm sort of a hermit crab." She took her glass too. "Until I met you, of course." Butterflies twirled and spun in her belly. "My favorite thing about our friendship, aside from having so much access to you, is our adventures. I'm really grateful that you take me out so much. Thank you, Rashad." The room felt warmer all of a sudden.

Rashad put his cup down. "It's no problem. I've been having such a ball getting to know you through all of them." He wiped his hands on his shirt then sat straighter. "What was your favorite place to go to growing up? Next time we meet, we should go there. I'll pick my favorite place too, and we'll stop by. It can be like going back in time."

"That's an amazing idea, Rashad. Do you ever run out of them?" India had never met someone so innovative.

He only laughed in response.

India dusted the crumbs off her hands. "For me, I liked the simpler things growing up. If our mom took us to the playground, I'd be happy the rest of that week." She sighed wistfully. "Those were the days. Sliding down slides, crawling through tunnels, and playing horses."

"Oh. Would you ever meet a random kid there and immediately make friends with them just to never see them again?" Rashad hit his knee as he cracked up. "That has to be an experience every kid has had."

India gave an exuberant nod and pointed. "Yes. That's happened to me too. I'd never been as outgoing as my little sister but I can count about two instances where Nevaeh, Kim, and I ran into someone there and decided to play with them. I'd never make the first move but I'd definitely go along with whatever we played." She found his hysterics comical. "What is it, Rashad? Do you have a wacky story you'd like to share?" He didn't need to say so, she already knew.

He finally composed himself. "I do." He crossed his left leg over his right. "Did I ever tell you about the time I met this kid who swore he was a pirate?"

India was already invested. "Please Rashad, tell me." She picked up her lemonade in preparation for this one.

They jumped from topic to topic as they conversed. Rashad spoke at length of his prankster reputation in high school while she outlined her rivalry with another gifted Scrabble player. They'd had vastly different school days but found common ground in awkward experiences. She laughed at his embarrassing stories while he laughed at hers. From there, they shared their dreams. What they hoped to accomplish before retirement and where they'd go once old age crept up on them. The two got lost in their life aspirations, thinking big unapologetically.

"And then," Rashad said, drawing out the moment so dramatically that India couldn't help but smile. He rested his shoulder on the backrest. They were face to face, staring deeply at each other. "I'll take the whole family on a cruise with me. Grandkids, great-grandkids, my old wife, and our children. It'd be like the ultimate family vacation. All sponsored by me. I'll die on board with everyone around me and tell them about all the great things I did in life and they'd thank me for allowing them to tag along on my last adventure." A look of pure content covered his face. "I know it's wishful thinking but I've always believed in putting my ambitions into the universe. Letting the heavens know what you want is the first step to achieving any dream." The playful flare of his eyes returned. "That's at least what I think."

India agreed. "There's some truth to that. My mom always said that whatever you speak becomes your reality. It's why she always encouraged us to speak kindly to ourselves. I think it's also how our brains work too. You have to voice your ideas to start taking steps to meet your goals." She leaned off the couch. They'd eaten every snack she'd brought out. India was filled. "So, you have the right attitude." Her heart did backflips as she contemplated her next move. They both had work tomorrow and it was getting late. She'd never forgive herself if he left before she said something. India needed to seize the moment. He was right where she needed him. "Rashad?"

He sat taller to stretch. "This was nice. It's been a while since I sat and talked to someone this long." He seemed to not have heard her. "I think I've thoroughly enjoyed my first stop by. Feels like home already." Rashad brushed his palms against his knees, seeming expectant.

India couldn't tell what he wanted. He patted his thighs idly while folding his lips and staring. "Rashad?" She tried a second time. This time, she projected her voice. He had to know. They gelled so well together. There'd never been another person she felt more at ease with. Rashad brought out sides of her she'd only shown Kim. The one person India trusted. With him, she was authentic. Herself at her purest. She'd never forgive herself if she didn't confess. India *liked* Rashad. More than a friend and perhaps deeper than a lover.

Her fear was that opening her heart would ruin them permanently. If Rashad didn't see her the same, their friendship would be ruined. A friendship she needed while Kim was far away. India couldn't see herself surviving without his company, optimism, and sweetness.

"What is it, India?" Rashad had been waiting in silence.

India was suddenly intimidated. His precious brown eyes struck fear through her core. Her words failed, and the suspense only grew. She was at fault for letting it swell, but India had no clue how to handle this. If only she'd spoken with Kim before tackling something so huge. Her friend would have a better grasp of what to do.

India told herself to relax. This situation shouldn't scare her. She wasn't a flustered teenage girl or a terrified tween. She'd lived and loved before Rashad, but somehow, he rendered her helpless and unable to speak.

She sat there as he stared in anticipation.

CHAPTER SIXTEEN

Shifting eyes, shivering lips, clenching fists, and the ever so slight rocking of her upper body. India was nervous, but why? Rashad had detected it earlier too; after they'd sat on her couch. There was something she had to say that made her like this.

He tried to guess what it could be. Did she have a secret she'd been hiding? Was there something she feared him discovering? Their friendship had blossomed since their first encounter. She shouldn't have feared him like she did now. Unless… what India had to say may affect what they'd built and change them forever. If so then he understood. He understood because Rashad himself had been holding off on revealing something too. But in his case, he'd been awaiting the perfect moment. Could this be it? Preah had said he'd know when to confess, and right now, his gut seemed sure.

"Wait India, before you open up…" And now *he* was nervous. Anxiety wrapped itself around his throat, hands, and feet. A cold sensation raced down his spine and made Rashad stiff. It was as if the universe wanted to stop him. He'd take it as a sign but his heart seemed certain. If he didn't speak now, he never would. "I have something to say."

She shrunk, now resembling a curious mouse. "Really?"

Rashad nodded. "But if you want to go first you can. I just thought I'd—"

"No, no you go ahead." India sighed quietly in relief. She seemed grateful for his interruption.

A slight smile twitched his lip corners at her reaction. If it meant her comfort, Rashad would go first. He had no problem taking one for the team. Someone had to be brave and take the next step. "Listen." He held her right hand. "I'm extremely happy I met you, but not only because it's been fun building our friendship but also because you've allowed me to discover the joys of liking someone." Her light brown eyes sparkled as they popped. "Yes. I mean liking someone as in having feelings for that person. And in my case that person is you." He could have said that more eloquently, but Rashad was scared. His heart and mind were in conflict. While his brain urged him to shut up and bask in what they already had, his gut and heart said otherwise. They told Rashad to hold her hand through transitioning.

When he reached for it, she reached for his as well.

"Rashad..." she said softly.

He shook his head. He needed to keep going or he'd never do this. "What I'm trying to say, I guess, is that I don't want to just be your friend, India. I like being your friend. I don't want to let that go. But I also want more."

She sucked in a breath. "When..."

He kept going. "I think I might have fallen for you the second you came to the shop in person for your daily ice cream. But back then, I wasn't sure." He squeezed her hand as her lips parted in what he viewed as stun. From here, it was hard to tell whether this stun was good, but he'd keep going. "Through spending time with you and discovering all your different sides, it became more and more apparent how I felt. You're not just gorgeous but also smart, funny, kind, gentle, and so many other great things. I haven't dated much in my time, but no woman has ever made me happier. We're like..." Rashad stroked her knuckle with his thumb. "Yin and Yang. At least to me. It feels like I need you." He took a deep breath and found it in him to meet her eyes. Hers seemed enamored as a smile crossed her face. This reaction was reassuring. Suddenly, his nerves weren't too much to bear. Preah was right. His timing had been perfect. "Anyway, if you're okay with it, I'd like to ask you out on a date. A romantic one between just the two of us. Our other dates were just us, but what I mean is that this date should be more intimate." Why were sentences suddenly difficult? He'd never worded anything more awkwardly. Where was his smooth talking now? She must have found him pathetic. "But we don't have to force it. We can slowly ease into the romance if you want. I'm not forcing you to say yes. It's completely okay if we take a while to adjust. Not that I'm putting words in your mouth. You know what?" He stroked his left arm as his face heated.

She giggled behind a curled finger.

"I'll let you give your answer," he said around the tightness in his chest.

There were two seconds of hesitation. Two moments where Rashad wasn't sure what would happen, but he knew that no matter what, his life would change.

As soon as India gave her answer.

Finally, India grinned. "It's a yes."

Rashad hopped to his feet triumphantly. "Alright!" The man sat back down, feeling over the moon. She seemed completely entertained by his actions. He didn't mind playing the fool for India. As long as she was happy, he'd be as well. "Was that what you wanted to say to me? You had something to say too."

"As a matter of fact, yes." India sighed with relief. "How did you know? Was I being obvious?"

"Not really. I just had a feeling you felt the same way but were too scared of possibly ruining our friendship to tell me," Rashad said. "It was how I felt for a while, so I saw it in how you hesitated. Trust me. Hiding feelings for someone is painful. And that pain is unmistakable."

"I see." She looked at her lap. "I didn't know there was a look to it, but thank you so much for recognizing and being brave enough to confess." India touched his knee. "Left up to me, we'd never evolve. I guess cowardice is a flaw of mine." She retracted her hand from his leg. "Though I'm trying to work on it."

Rashad reached back for it. "Don't call yourself a coward when you aren't." He placed their joined hands on his knee. "I recall you mentioning how much you prefer staying in than going out. Yet for the past few weeks, you've gone out with me countless times. A coward would've stayed in their comfort zone even if they wanted to try new things." He watched as she slowly lifted her head. "And trust me, anyone would have found it hard to say how they felt. It's one of the most difficult things you can do. If I were you, I wouldn't beat myself up."

She tightened her grip on his hold. "Thanks for saying that." India faced the TV in uncertainty. It was like there was something she wanted but was unsure of how to ask. Something from him that was difficult to acquire. Thinking of it longer led Rashad to change his mind. Maybe what India desired wasn't hard to request but tricky. "No. Awkward," he whispered.

India perked up when he spoke. "Hm?"

Rashad flicked his wrist dismissively. "Nothing. I was talking to myself."

"Oh okay. Well, we should plan our date now. Our first real date." Her eyes wouldn't stop glancing at his lips.

Rashad couldn't believe his luck. Did she also want a kiss? Was that it? Was that something that they should do now that the feelings were out in the open? She wanted a kiss? Were they ready? Rashad might have missed his chance just now. Now she'd asked a question he couldn't ignore. "Sure. There's tons we can do. Like take a walk or see a movie."

India scooted closer. "All the things we've done before?" She intertwined their fingers on his lap. He could see she was waiting for the perfect chance to peck his lips. There was still hesitation in her motions but Rashad could help with that. If the right time arose and she stumbled, he'd lean in and take the lead. But he had to time this perfectly. Just like when he'd poured out his soul. If he let his heart guide him, their first kiss would be magical.

"If you want, we can kick things up a notch," Rashad said smoothly. He kept an eye on how her body behaved. She'd stopped lip-watching to stare him head-on. This may mean she'd opted to abandon the kiss, leaving Rashad the sole seeker of this showing of affection. "Take you out somewhere nice. There's an amazing restaurant in Peachwood we can go to. It'll be my treat if you say yes." He softened his voice to send a message. He yearned to taste those sweet lips. They seemed so inviting, gentle, and pure.

India seemed enticed. "Sounds amazing, but I actually liked your suggestion. We should keep being us." She moved their linked hands to her thigh. "If we make an effort to change, then we won't be ourselves. I was completely okay with doing everything we'd done already. Just with a bit extra added in." She shrugged shyly and smiled with evident cheek.

"What kind of extra?" He wanted her to say it. To outline all the great experiences they could share as a couple. Things he'd wished to do but never could. Now with no restrictions, they'd have more fun. They'd already started by holding hands and sitting close. He wished for even more tender interactions between them.

India giggled, tilting her head. "You know, like holding hands when we walk, feeding one another, matching, piggyback rides." She had a good laugh when she finished. "I'm just exaggerating but you asked. If it's too corny, we don't have to do that stuff. I'm just excited at the possibilities." She seemed energized suddenly, sitting upright and bouncing in place. "If we go to the movies again, this time, we can order one of those jumbo popcorns for couples. Do you remember seeing that on the menu?"

Rashad had already started fantasizing about her suggestions. He'd never gone all out in a relationship but wouldn't mind if she asked him to. While matching seemed kind of ridiculous, he'd be all for it. All India needed to do was say the word and he'd purchase identical beanies for them. "I remember those. They came in pink. The pink popcorn bags were so cute." He chortled then snapped his fingers. "Yes. We can finally do that. They thought we were together when we first went anyway. This time, they won't be surprised that we are."

"Exactly." India applauded him softly, cheering at this incredible idea. "But really, we don't have to change too much. It's the same India and Rashad but more intimate. Closer than before." She lowered her face in apparent fascination at their hands. Soon she was humming a love song.

Rashad picked up the tune. He knew it. It was a classic he'd heard as a child. If he wasn't mistaken, his mother loved this song. She'd labeled it her favorite, but with her, all love songs were highly favored. He guessed songs were to her how he saw ice cream. "India."

She raised her face, brown eyes calling him close.

As if by instinct, he touched her chin and rested his lips on hers.

Rashad pecked them once, then drew back. He'd closed his eyes, but only for a second. Now they were open, peering at her.

India's remained shut. She seemed to be waiting or reflecting.

He got scared. Was it not what she'd anticipated? Had he read her actions wrong? He knew he should have waited. Now everything was ruined. India now found him repulsive and wanted nothing to do with him. Any smart person would have asked, but Rashad went in. He went in with no permission, and now—.

She fit her lips back on his.

Surprised, Rashad's eyes bulged. He blinked as she kissed him with passion. It wasn't as deep as other kisses but found a middle ground that worked. As if to send a message that she was ready and eager to explore him.

His heart pounded as he responded to the action by closing his eyes and holding her face. They smooched for six seconds until she pulled back. He felt hypnotized as her hooded eyes made contact. Rashad could hardly breathe. He tried to catch his breath but had severe difficulty. It was official, she'd taken his breath away. Suffocating had never felt more riveting. As for his heart? It beat like a drum. He sensed it in every part of him. From his veins to his limbs and even his lips quivered by what they'd shared. Was this the preview to what they would be? If so, he was sold. Rashad had enjoyed every second they'd kissed for. Like kissing India had brought him to heaven then back.

She flipped some misplaced hair off her shoulder then touched her lips with two fingers. "Too much?" Listening to that timid little voice was strange after she'd blessed him with such impactful affection. She seemed so shy but just now had taken charge. He'd let her lead the awesome exchange and lead him she did.

"No. Thank you." The words felt appropriate after something so great. "I don't think I've ever been kissed like that." Her taste remained on his lips. He hadn't realized she was wearing flavored lip gloss. It tasted like cherries, sour but sweet. He licked it and held his lips too. They had a brief stare-off before he smiled.

She smiled back, and they both started snickering. They laughed as if they'd gotten away with something and maybe they did. Just now, they'd shared an incredible encounter that only they knew of. It was just him and her in this small living room that felt like its own world.

Rashad chose right to open his heart. If he'd held back longer, they wouldn't have kissed. And he wouldn't have known how perfect they were for each other. They hadn't even had their first date, but it was clear to him that this would last.

"It's getting late, but I wanted to show you something before you went home." India got up and rushed to her TV stand. "This movie is only an hour so it won't keep you. If you want, I can let you bring it home to watch in your spare time." She knelt beside her shelf of movies.

Rashad didn't care what time it was. "No, pop it in now. I like movies." He rubbed his hands as she found it. "What is it about?" He got to his feet to have a look.

India explained the plot without giving spoilers. She grinned while saying why she liked it then put in the DVD. From there, she instructed Rashad to sit as it started. Now, the excited India, raced to the kitchen for more snacks.

"Let me help you in there." Rashad paused the movie.

They stood side by side while rummaging the pantry. As they did, he watched her every move, completely mystified by her presence.

He had been so afraid of this moment.

And now, he couldn't remember why.

CHAPTER SEVENTEEN

There was something about this Sunday afternoon that felt more special than others. Butterflies circled flowers, while tweeting birds sang from towering trees that lined the trail. Its soft dirt was like a pillow under India's feet. She couldn't recall a time when she'd ventured this far into nature. The bustling streets of Sweetgum were now far off.

"And you said that your friend would walk here all the time?" Rashad didn't look fazed by their long journey. They'd been hiking for thirty minutes, but their constant conversations made it seem like less.

India herself was still bursting with energy. Before setting off, a park ranger had provided them with advice on how to approach hiking. They hadn't chosen a steep trail but a long one. Through dating for a month, she and Rashad had discovered their love for lengthy walks. It gave them time to talk and catch up while exercising. Usually, at the end of these walk dates, they'd grab a bite to eat as a reward for their efforts. She'd grown to love not only exercising with Rashad but everything else too. Whether it be helping him at the shop, farm, or even with organizing his own DVDs, India loved their time together.

Transitioning between being friends to lovers had gone swimmingly. They'd started with a few more traditionally romantic dates before going back to their more carefree outings. The dinners and carriage rides hadn't been too different from when they'd hang out prior to dating. Apart from kissing and hand-holding, she and Rashad had been just as laidback as they'd been as friends. Nothing had become awkward or forced.

Over these past few weeks, they'd also spent more time together. She'd tagged along with Rashad's family to the town cookout where they'd had barbecue chicken and potato salad. She'd even cheered on his niece while she performed with her xylophone for the town talent show. So much had happened, but one thing India would never forget was how Rashad's brother won the annual pie-eating contest with ease. From that day, she'd respected professional football players even more. The man had credited his athlete's appetite for his victory.

"Yes. She actually met her fiancé on these trails. The story is pretty dramatic but sweet. They're off traveling right now but plan on getting married while they're away. It's amazing that they have their own reality TV show, but I'm a bit sad that they won't be marrying here in Sweetgum." India took a swig of water, then put the bottle back in her bag. They both carried backpacks with essentials for this mini adventure. "But I guess getting married somewhere foreign could be fun too. A new and interesting place. What do you think?" They'd also spent time together in the shop. Together, they'd created the most unique ice cream flavor known to man. A tasty blend of almonds and chocolate had been the result of an all-nighter spent at the parlor. They'd thrown in tons of organic food coloring to get a fun theme and had made star-shaped sprinkles mandatory with every cup. Naturally, it instantly became a hit. Rashad had thanked her a thousand times, but India knew that both their efforts had been necessary to accomplish this feat.

Since then, they'd practically spent every day together. She'd kept him in check in terms of putting order to his belongings, and he'd given her all the gentle nudges she needed to venture out of her comfort zone. If it wasn't for him, this date wouldn't be possible. An outside hiking date wasn't something India would be keen on in the past. But after trying so many new activities with Rashad, she'd been ready for something outlandish. Once they arrived at the trail's end, they'd have a picnic. According to the ranger who'd guided them before, a picnic bench and table would await them when they got there. Breaking for snacks after walking wasn't so uncommon.

"Of course. A lot of folks travel far for their weddings just for the new experience. I'm sure that Kim will be happy with her choice." Rashad slushed the water in his squeeze water bottle around, then squirted some into his mouth. "Getting married somewhere far and surrounded by nature seems perfect for her and Malik."

India couldn't agree more. She sighed in content while staring at the sky. The way the tree branches threatened to hide its blueness satisfied her. She especially loved when small birds soared high with open wings. They looked like angels with the light at their backs. "If it wasn't so hot, I'd say we should do this next week too." As if to remind her of the heat, two drops of sweat rolled down her back. They seeped through her tank top and soaked the fabric. "But unfortunately, this summer has reached record-breaking levels of heat, so I can't say that." She smiled at the sweaty Rashad who'd just dabbed his forehead with a towel.

Rashad dried his neck with the towel too. "You could. We'd just have to take a horse next time. The rangers have a lot of those at their cabin." He winked.

"Riding a horse?" India guffawed at the idea. That may be much for a simple date. They'd already gotten the more romantic dating activities out of the way. There surely wasn't any need for that. "You know when Kim first met Malik, he'd been on a horse."

"Yes. I remember when you told me." Rashad crinkled his brow at her as they slowed down.

India could feel the heat rising, and her energy depleting. It seemed the exertion was finally catching up. "I did?"

The cheery Rashad nodded, still as upbeat as ever. "Just now you acted like I didn't know their whole story, but I do." He giggled. "You told me about ten minutes into our walk." He pulled on his bag straps to adjust the way his backpack hung. "It seems this date location is bringing back tons of memories of Kim."

India thought back and realized he was right. "Oh boy." She hit her forehead and groaned, ceasing her strides. "Have I been rambling about Kim without knowing again?" She'd done so at least five times in his presence. Rashad never complained when she spoke of her best friend, but India was sure it annoyed him. Their dates were not the time to whine and moan about missing Kim. Whenever India brought Kim up, she'd end by saying she missed her. That had to get old rather quickly.

"Hey, what did I say?" He stopped too and touched both her shoulders. "It's not rambling if you're saying meaningful things." Rashad shook her gently, then slid his hands down to hers.

India soaked up every ounce of comfort from his palms. She placed his left hand on her cheek and shut her eyes. "I know you always say that but it's the only word I can come up with. Something else may be more fitting, but I don't know."

He pulled her fingers to his lips and kissed them. Rashad let go of one hand to hold just the other. They now traveled hand in hand, strolling leisurely. "If you want to talk about Kim, you can. I like listening to how happy she makes you." She heard the genuine glee in his tone. "That's what best friends should do."

India's sigh was different this time. She looked sadly at the ground. "I know, but when I start talking, I wound up missing her, and things turn sad quickly. I really hate downing the mood." Through life, she'd learned to suppress her emotions for that same reason. Rashad tended to be understanding when her gloomier side made an appearance, but India still made an effort to sustain a certain level of brightness around him.

"It's better to express yourself," Rashad said easily. He looked ahead in what looked like wonder. The guy whistled when the chatty birds tweeted, and they actually responded.

India watched in amazement for a second, and at the same time she did, the lightest breeze blew against her overheated skin. "You're right, but I don't like being sad. We should talk about something else." She smiled at the way their hands linked. "Like how you'll be meeting my family tomorrow."

"Yes. That's something fun. It's like the next big step in our relationship." Though Rashad seemed ecstatic to finally meet her folks, India sensed the slightest unease in how he expressed himself. It was in the way that he twitched whenever they talked about it. "So it's just going to be your mom and sister, right?" He went on.

India stopped staring to answer. "Neveah will most likely bring her fiancé. You know him, don't you? When I brought him up last time you mentioned that."

Rashad whistled again, and an unseen bird replied.

India paused in awe.

"I don't know him that well, but I'm familiar with his work. His dance studio is pretty popular. My sister had once considered taking my niece to some classes. But she's too young right now." Rashad moved his head from left to right as two small birds flew from one tree branch to another. "In the future, I'm sure he'll make a good teacher for her."

India could testify that Sean indeed was great at teaching. "He has a lot of patience. I would know since my sister was his student. Dancing was sort of her only weak point, but he took his time with her and now she's an expert." She rubbed her chin as they reached a wooden sign shaped like an arrow. It was pointing to an area ahead. A table and bench setup to the left of where the trail bent sideways. It seemed steeper terrain lay ahead of this path. "Okay, I misspoke. She's not an expert, but was able to dance well enough at her best friend's wedding. We were all surprised that she pulled it off. I'm not exaggerating when I say she had two left feet." The sight of their destination brought India great relief. She hadn't noticed how far they'd traveled.

"Interesting. I'll stick a pin in that." Rashad pulled the towel from his backpack and dabbed his damp forehead. He smiled at the picnic table then faced India. "Shall we?"

"We shall." India held his hand as they proceeded.

CHAPTER EIGHTEEN

"It's just dinner." He had to persistently remind himself of this the following night.

Rashad put his truck in park outside of India's apartment building. He'd been here on many occasions but never under these circumstances. "It's just dinner with the most important people in her life." He gulped at his reflection in the rear-view mirror.

The pressure was definitely on.

He'd done well at acting nonchalant when India spoke of him dining with her family, but deep down, Rashad was terrified. She got along so well with his. It would be awful if he somehow turned off her mom and sister after she'd done so well at fitting in with his folks. "That'd make future Thanksgivings really awkward." He broke his collar in the mirror.

Being likable was part of his charm. From since childhood, Rashad had always been a social butterfly. He got along with everyone at school and made friends easily. Events like dinners or meeting new people never usually intimidated him, but tonight was different. This was *India's* family. He just *had* to ensure that they liked him. If something went awry, it might ruin their relationship.

Rashad patted his cheeks to shake this terrible mindset.

Reminding himself of his likability had been his way of easing his nerves. How did it wind up having the opposite effect just now? He supposed that this was just testament to his nervousness. "But there's no need for that." As long as he was polite, kind, and attentive, India's mother would certainly like him. The same went for her sister and brother-in-law. Nevaeh hadn't yet gotten married, but India had already given Sean this title. Therefore, Rashad referred to him the same way.

He took a deep breath and popped his door open. The sidewalk was clear due to the time of night. This allowed Rashad to psyche himself up without fear of judgment. He walked over to one of the back doors and swung it open, practicing what he'd say after meeting India's mom. India had described her as meek. With that information, he'd decided she was India in an older woman's body. Thinking along these lines somewhat helped him with calming down, but Rashad's anxiety was still prominent.

The heat of his homemade mac and cheese seeped through the glass tray he'd put it in. Rashad shut the door with his foot and placed the tray on top of his car. He locked his car then lifted the tray again, still trying to convince himself that there was nothing to be afraid of.

Ding.

He stepped off the elevator and entered a carpeted corridor. Rashad watched the foil he'd placed over the macaroni. Maybe India's mom wasn't someone to worry about. Her sister sounded more unpredictable than the tender woman who'd raised his girlfriend. According to India, Nevaeh was everything India wasn't. Where India was shy, Nevaeh was bold. Where India was tender, Nevaeh could be more abrasive. He'd come across all sorts of personality types in his lifetime. Nevaeh's audacious tendencies normally wouldn't frighten him, but in the setting of a family dinner, it may pose a problem.

Walking this hall alone gave Rashad a sense of isolation. The rooms behind the doors seemed oddly quiet. Was anyone home?

She'd told him her apartment number so Rashad was on the lookout for that. It was apartment fifty at the end of the hall. He had a long way to go and plenty of time to ponder. If Nevaeh somehow already disliked him, she'd by no means shy away from showing it. He'd expect her to be more responsible than that, but Rashad couldn't be sure. Some people didn't view such behavior as unacceptable.

He shook his head as he neared her door. Thinking along these lines wasn't healthy. Tonight would be fun. He'd do what he did best and bring smiles to everyone's faces. From India's mom to Sean would leave this occasion happy all due to Rashad's efforts. Nothing would go wrong, and if by some miracle it did, he'd look past the negative and transform it into a positive. He was good at that. Rashad needed to remind himself of his strengths going into this.

"India, it's me." He knocked twice with one hand then waited. Preah had picked out his outfit. It was just a simple polo and jeans, but the clothes were new. They looked fresh, and he'd touched up his haircut for tonight too. He'd do anything to help his chances.

The golden doorknob twisted, and a few seconds later, India was staring right at his face. "Rashad!" She stopped herself from hugging him once spotting what he held. "You really made the mac and cheese?" She seemed touched. "You didn't have to. I know you're busy with work."

Suddenly, Rashad's fears melted away. Something about India put his woes to rest. "I wanted to." He heard talking in the kitchen and made out the rest of India's guests standing by the table. This amazing aroma struck out to him, too. It seemed they'd be in for quite the feast tonight. "What? Did someone else prepare this dish?" He entered when she made room for him to do so.

India's heels clicked against the floor as she led him in further. She too smelled incredible. It complemented her look of elegance this evening. A frilly pink blouse was worn on her upper half. Some fitted jeans hugged her legs and ankles. "Nevaeh may have prepared a small tray but it's fine." She smiled over her shoulder as they met everyone in the kitchen. "The more food the better." With that, she seized his dish.

"Rashad. It's so great to meet you. India's shared so many great things about you." A slender woman wearing a sleeveless denim dress embraced him without warning. She gave Rashad a gentle squeeze before pulling away. "She didn't mention you could cook though." Her hair was done in twists that stopped over her shoulders. There were red-rimmed spectacles resting on the bridge of her nose. "That mac and cheese smells appetizing."

Rashad didn't need an introduction. "Thank you, Ms. Carr. It's made with love and effort." He watched as India rested it on the table along with the other sealed trays and plates. Things looked all set for mealtime already. A plate and cutlery were assigned to every seat. "And might I just say now that it is so good to meet you too." He held out his hand right as the two other guests approached. "You must be…"

"Nevaeh. India's sister." Nevaeh wore a fancy top and jeans just like India. She'd done her hair in a bun on top of her head. "I've seen you around town, but I believe that this might be the first time we're formally meeting." She smiled but the corners of her lips shook.

Rashad ignored this oddity to take her hand. "Yes. But it's an honor to meet the sister of my beautiful girlfriend." India put her arms around him when he spoke. Looking closely at Nevaeh allowed him to see their resemblance. Their mother had a similar face too. It was all in the eyes. They shared the same shaped eyes.

"It's an honor to meet you too. I trust that you're a good guy. Seems so so far, but you know, first impressions can sometimes be misleading." Nevaeh choked on a brief laugh while shaking his hand longer than necessary.

Rashad glanced at India, who'd furrowed her brows slightly. This reaction was short-lived since Nevaeh's fiancé took his hand next.

"Nice to meet you, Rashad. I'm Sean. I think we've met once or twice before." Sean's outfit seemed more formal than anyone else's. His black shirt had buttons and a collar. "Did you attend the Sweetgum Business Owners Association meeting that time?"

Rashad responded with a nod. "I did. I met you there too. That's great. I think that my sister also tried to enroll my niece into your classes, but we decided to let her wait until she's six." He drew back his hand as Sean snapped his fingers.

"Yes. That's a good idea. I usually advise that kids start young, but sometimes it's frustrating to learn certain moves before they hit six." Sean placed his hands on his hips. "But I will be looking forward to seeing her once she gets a little older."

"I can't wait either. I'm sure watching her dance will be adorable. And of course, good for character building." Rashad received a friendly pat from Sean who voiced his agreement.

India clapped. "Okay great. We're all acquainted, so we can go ahead and take a seat to start eating." She pulled out a chair toward the table's longer side for Rashad. "You'll be right next to me." She patted the cushion.

As India's mom took the seat at the head and Nevaeh and Sean settled across from him and India, Rashad sat. "I honestly wouldn't want it any other way." He beamed at the chuckle that came from India's mom. "Who made what?" He pointed to the varying delicacies before him. "Because it all looks absolutely fantastic."

India just sat at his side. "I prepared the beans, rice, and meat while Nevaeh and Sean made the Shepherd's Pie, mac and cheese, and fish." She gestured to each dish with an open palm.

"Wow." He comically sniffed. "It all smells really good. You didn't tell me cooking ran in the family." Rashad gave India a slight poke with his elbow.

"I wouldn't say we're *great* cooks, but we do try. We know our way around the kitchen." Nevaeh picked up a spoon to dish out her rice while Sean used a pair of tongs to put meat on his plate.

Rashad went ahead and picked food out for himself. In no time, they were all doing just that. "I think you should definitely give yourselves more credit. This food seems professional from where I'm sitting." He faced India. "But I know that some of you don't settle for anything less than perfection."

India giggled unassumingly. "You need to let the taste be the judge of that."

When their plates were filled and everyone had made headway in their meals, Sean had started questioning India and Rashad on how they got together.

"I think it was fate," India said. She scraped a portion of baked beans onto her fork. "We both just naturally fell for each other after spending time together as friends. I'm just glad Rashad did what I couldn't and told me when his feelings shifted into something deeper."

India's mother raised her brows. "I can imagine the tension you must have felt." She fidgeted to demonstrate what she meant. "That's a scary thing to do when you have a nice friendship. You never know how opening up can affect it." She used her knife to saw off a slice of turkey on her plate.

"Exactly. I think that's what we were both thinking." Rashad had taken four slices of mac and cheese. The blend of cheese and seasoning had been so tasty that he'd already devoured them. Only one remained. "But bottling up your emotions is more harmful than potentially ruining something." As he shared, the penetrating gaze of Nevaeh grew more apparent. Her seat was directly across from his. While her fiancé seemed genuinely intrigued by their story, Nevaeh looked untrusting. Not of the events that led to his relationship but of Rashad himself. She looked to be struggling with holding back. She must have wanted to ask him something. "But that's our story." Perhaps Rashad could be of assistance. "Please, I'd be more than happy to know how the two of you got to know each other." He met Sean's eyes. "One second you and I were single pringles together and the next I hear you're tying the knot."

Sean chewed his food behind a persistent grin. He grabbed a napkin to wipe off his lips then crumpled it. "Incredible, isn't it?" The man just swallowed what he'd been munching. As if by instinct, he lifted his glass. "Just goes to show you that miracles can happen to anyone." As his eyes connected to the woman beside him, they gradually filled with unmistakable adoration. Rashad would know what that looked like. He gave India the same stare all the time.

Nevaeh finally backed off Rashad to smile at Sean. She played with her rice by swishing it around with the fork she held. "You could say our meeting was fate too." A dreamy sigh expelled from her lungs. "And now we're focusing on planning the wedding." She suddenly gasped and slammed her hand on the table. "India, did I tell you it's a double wedding with Court?"

"Really?" India stopped mid-way of putting a fork full of turkey in her mouth.

"Yes!" It amazed Rashad how quickly she flipped from internally interrogating him to clapping. "We just thought it would be best since we got engaged around the same time and are already so close. Why not just have a double wedding?" She rocked herself back and forth in uncontainable joy. "I don't think it's ever been done before either." All motions came to a halt as she framed her cheeks with her hands. "Have you ever heard of anyone having a joined wedding in Sweetgum with their closest friend?"

Rashad preferred her hyper side to how she'd been before. "So what's the theme?" He'd encourage this overzealous behavior by asking more.

"Everlasting sunsets, right?" asked the older woman at the table. She'd just pressed the rim of her glass to her bottom lip. The question was almost swallowed by her juice.

Nevaeh clasped her hands on the table. "No. We're still in the idea exchanging phase but we are looking at something that pertains to the sun."

"How about Infinite Sunrise? And you can have it out of town on a beach right before dawn. It can start out at night but spill into morning." Rashad liked planning activities and other occasions that brought forth true happiness. He asked India for her thoughts.

She scratched her head. "It certainly sounds unique but also a bit demanding for guests who'd have to wake up at an odd hour to attend." India's shoulders jerked as she laughed. "Can you imagine waking up at three a.m. to attend a wedding at four?"

Rashad now saw the flaws in his idea. "There's plenty of time to decide that." He found himself giggling with his girlfriend.

"We'd actually planned on having the ceremony earlier but had to push things back due to the plan to merge it with Courtney's." Sean made a gesture where his fingers linked to indicate merger. He helped himself to more meat after illustrating this. "I personally don't mind not having a theme, but it all depends on what Nevaeh thinks is best. She's the expert at event planning. I trust her with this more than anyone else."

The mother beamed at her end of the table. "Oh yes. And her business is already gaining lots of traffic." She clapped to a beat while moving up and down in place.

"That's incredible. So you're a professional event planner?" Rashad cut his shepherd's pie into quarters.

"She's in the beginning stages of becoming one," India clarified.

Nevaeh hadn't touched her food since filling her plate. She coyly shrugged and looked away. "You could say I'm a full-blown event planner. There's nothing wrong with that. I mean, I've gotten a few clients already so it's going well." At last, she picked up her fork. "If you or a friend or even someone you know needs a pro to set up a special event for them. Just give me a call," she punctuated her point, making a fake phone with her fingers.

Rashad thanked the heavens that she'd relaxed off her suspicions. "I think I will."

"Speaking of friends, who do you normally mingle with in town, Rashad?" Nevaeh cocked her head sideways. "I see you around, but you're usually always at the ice cream parlor." She picked around at her food with the teeth of her fork. "Who are you with when you're not there?"

The question caught him off-guard, but Rashad didn't stay stunned for too long. "Sometimes me and my staff have outings where we gallivant around town on a Friday, but I don't think you'd know all of them." He stirred his cup of orange juice. While his plate was practically empty, Nevaeh still had much more to consume. "Let's see." He reclined and crossed his arms while staring upward. The central light nearly blinded him. "There's Joel—"

"Joel?" Nevaeh seemed disturbed. "Didn't he get into an accident recently?" She clutched a confused Sean's arm. "He's a reckless driver."

India sat forward then. "Hey, what are you saying, Nev?" She continuously turned from Rashad to her sister. "How would you know if Joel was in an accident? And if he was, why would you automatically assume that?"

Rashad drank half his glass of juice. "He was in a very small accident during a delivery once, but he honestly wasn't to blame for what happened. I'm surprised word spread far enough to reach you." It shouldn't have come as a shock. Though this had taken place a few years ago, when something unusual occurred in their humble town, people talked. "It was about five years ago." He filled in India and her mom since they looked perplexed.

India's mom snapped her fingers. "Oh yes. I remember an incident with an ice-cream van and a motorcycle. Was he injured?"

"No. The truck just sustained a few minor damages."

Nevaeh stabbed her mac and cheese with her fork. "Have any of your other friends been involved in accidents?"

India subtly shook her head, raising her upper eyelids to convey a message to Nevaeh. "I'm sure they weren't. And if they were, it'd be unfortunate. Not something to accuse them of."

"Who's accusing who?" Nevaeh left her fork in the mac and cheese. Rashad couldn't see, but her hands appeared to stroke her lower belly. The tips of her brows met in a frown conveying earnest concern. "I'm just trying to get to know Rashad's friends." She simmered down after sighing. "Sorry if I came off a little strong just now. I've been told my personality is intense." The feet of her chair grazed the floor in a jarring scrape as she backed up her seat.

Rashad, ever relaxed, forgave her. "Don't even worry about it. Sometimes I get excited and come off the same way. India can tell you all about it." He decided to rope her into the conversation.

"I wouldn't say that. You use discretion very well." India's fork was filled with a collection of rice, beans, and shepherd's pie.

"Thank you." Rashad placed a palm on his chest. "My mom always said to think of others before myself growing up." He faced a curious Sean. "It was how she stopped me from pressuring other kids into playing with me on the playground."

Sean made an 'o' with his lips then laughed. "That's adorable. Sometimes energetic kids need guidance." Everything on his plate had been eaten. "Ms. Carr, I'm sure you have tons of stories of keeping this one in check." He gestured an arm to Nevaeh.

As her mother wheezed on inaudible laughter, Nevaeh stroked her tummy. She refused to peel her eyes away from Rashad, who tried his hardest to avoid connecting eyes with her. From his experience, ignoring was best when it came to nosy characters. Although in Nevaeh's case, he could tell that something else was at play.

India joined her mother's laughter after the woman shared some stories. "I think that most children appreciated her friendliness. I know for sure that it helped me with loosening up from time to time. She honestly—"

"I'm sorry to interrupt, but Rashad," said Nevaeh.

"Yup?" Rashad could practically feel India's discomfort. He amped up his nonchalance to send a message. Nevaeh's interrogation wasn't as upsetting to him as India thought.

Nevaeh folded her lips as if fighting the urge to speak. Eventually, her urge won, and she blurted out a question. "I heard that when you're seen with your young niece, she's often crying. Why is that?" She clasped her fingers on the table.

"*Nevaeh,*" Sean, India, and the mother said simultaneously. They used the same cadence to convey shock.

"What?" Nevaeh parted her arms genuinely. "It's just a question."

Rashad didn't make a big stink out of it. "Destiny can throw tantrums from time to time, but I can assure you that most of the time when I babysit for Preah, she's an angel." He'd use this prompt to speak on his sweet little niece. "You know how kids always have phases?" Sean already seemed intrigued. "Well, right now, all Destiny can talk about is—"

"Is there anything that you're doing which might contribute to her constant tantrums?" Nevaeh massaged her lower belly again. Everything from her shifting eyes to constant blinking told Rashad that his suspicions were true. She wasn't at all malicious about questioning him.

India got up before he could answer.

"Everything alright?" Rashad asked.

India touched his shoulder affectionately. "Yes. I just need to have a short word with my sister," her eyes caught Nevaeh's meaningfully, and she signaled to the living room with her head.

Nevaeh's stun was short-lived. Without much protest, she rose and trailed India to the living room.

In their absence, Sean put down his fork with a shaking head. "I am *so* sorry about all the questions." He dug his nails into his scalp. "You were about to mention how your niece is in a phase, right? Well, about now, Nev's going through something similar, so please just bear with her. She means no harm," he gently clasped his hands and gave a slight bow.

"Yes. It's not that she's suspicious of you. It's really just something she can't help at the moment." The mother flashed him an apologetic stare with a hand over her chest.

Rashad raised his hands. "It's completely fine. No. I understand. You guys don't need to apologize. I think I have a clue of where this is stemming from. I'd had to deal with someone in a similar boat as Nevaeh." He turned around to peep into the living room. From here, he couldn't hear a word said between the sisters, but India's gesticulation told him she was mad. He spotted a few head shakes from Nevaeh as well as sharp arm motions. The last thing he wanted was for a quarrel to ensue on such an important night. There was no need for any confrontations. "Hold on." He rose from his seat to check on them.

❧✿❧

WHEN RASHAD WENT to check on the sisters, Nevaeh had just taken a breath before her next argument. "Is everything alright?" He stood akimbo once they were aware of his presence.

India smiled tightly with joined hands. "Yes. Nevaeh here was just about to agree on what to say for her apology." She aimed the tip of her fingers at the one she referred to. "Right Nev? Rashad's here now, so why not get it over with?"

Nevaeh seemed reluctant, but a single sigh indicated that she released the chip that had settled on her shoulder. "Okay, fine." She looked away. "I'm sorry for questioning you like that. I honestly didn't mean to come off as if I found you untrustworthy. It's me, not you. So again, I'm so sorry if I made you uneasy during your first dinner with our family." She slumped her shoulders when their eyes finally met.

"I'll say what I told Sean and your mom. It's okay. I understand, and there's really no hard feelings." Rashad could tell India had been firm while confronting her. She wasn't normally one to speak out or chastise others, so Nevaeh's behavior must have definitely gotten to her. "How far along are you?" He asked his girlfriend's downcast sister.

Nevaeh's brows crinkled, and India's did the same. "Pardon?" They asked together. He'd never seen them look more alike.

"In your pregnancy. How far along are you? First trimester, right?" He went on, not letting their confusion throw him off.

Nevaeh gave India a questioning stare, then blinked at Rashad.

"How do you know that I'm pregnant?" She whipped her face back to India. "I thought you said you didn't tell anyone."

"I didn't. We all agreed to keep it among family." India stepped closer to Rashad. "Did something give it away?" She asked with crossed arms.

Rashad nodded. "Her mini-interrogations at the table told me everything." He smiled. "My sister was the same when she was pregnant. There wasn't a soul she didn't thoroughly question when we first introduced them to her. She insisted on conducting mini-investigations on any new person I brought forward. Her tact completely disappeared, and her personality was more like Sherlock Holmes than the Preah I knew." Memories of Preah going out of her way to inquire about newly hired employees resurfaced in his mind. They made Rashad laugh. "I just took it as her way of ensuring any potential new faces in her baby's life were good influences. I totally understand why you did what you did, so don't let it eat at you." He winked.

Nevaeh seemed to not have fully recovered from his knowing. "Wow. Um…" She faced India.

India looked less concerned and more amazed. "That's quite the assumption to make, though. Nevaeh could have been prying for other reasons, but you somehow knew for sure that it was that one."

"Are you sure you didn't overhear it from someone? Do people around town know?" Nevaeh folded her hands anxiously. "We really don't want this getting out, but it's not impossible that someone caught on and started spreading rumors. Are you sure this is just your own intuition talking?" She looked sick at the prospect of others catching wind of this.

Rashad could respect her wishes for privacy. Pregnancies were a complicated phenomenon. "Trust me. It really is just my own assessment. The second you started, I saw my sister in you. There was a chance I could have been wrong, but it was one of those cases where your gut just knows." He tapped his stomach for emphasis. "Don't worry. No one knows apart from me and your family."

"Trust Rashad, Nev. I highly doubt that word spread. Don't let your paranoia get to you." India put a comforting hand on Nevaeh's shoulder. "It's not good for the forming baby."

At that, Nevaeh inhaled deeply while rubbing her temples. "Yes, I know, I know." She sighed. "Okay. I believe you." Nevaeh made eye contact with one hand, rubbing her shoulder. "But you can't tell a soul about it." She placed a protective hand on her belly. "We need to see how things go first." A small smile emerged on her lips. "But I guess I'm preaching to the choir. Your sister went through everything I'm going through now, so you're more than familiar with what it's like to be in my position."

"I was just about to say that." Rashad appreciated her pleasantness. They'd started off on the wrong foot, but now, things were looking up. "I wish you all the best. If all goes well, you'll have a beautiful addition to your family. I can imagine the very prospect is exciting for all of you. When my sister was with child, I was over the moon." He clenched an ecstatic fist to indicate what he meant.

India bounced beside a giggling Nevaeh. "Trust me. We're all praying for the best. It is exciting. Wouldn't you agree, Nev?" She tapped her sister's back.

"Yes, of course!" Nevaeh exclaimed. "I'm bouncing off the walls but simultaneously terrified." They all had a good laugh at that one. "But yes. It sure is exhilarating." She held her stomach again. "And to answer your question, yes, I *am* in my first trimester. About to head into my second. Soon, I'll be showing."

Rashad nodded. "Those days are some of the best parts of it." He looked to the kitchen. "I'm glad we had this talk. Sorry for springing up that I caught on so suddenly. I can imagine it to be frightening. Especially since this is our first time meeting." He scratched the back of his head.

"Ah, it's alright. You're India's man, so it's not as bad as an outsider realizing." Nevaeh faced the kitchen. "We should head back, shouldn't we?"

"Oh yes." India took Rashad by the hand. "There's still a lot to eat, and I even bought dessert." She grinned at him with squinted eyes. "You'll never guess what it is."

But he could. Rashad preferred hearing it from her, so he acted clueless. "Whatever could it be?"

India's eyes twinkled. "Ice cream!"

CHAPTER NINETEEN

The next day was Saturday, and India still hadn't gotten over the events of Friday night. She had hoped for a smooth dinner between her boyfriend and her family, but things had gotten bumpy rather quickly. Rashad was as sweet as a cherry about everything, but India would have preferred if that little interrogation hadn't taken place at all. No matter how understanding someone was, something like that was bound to stir anyone during their first meeting with family. Such an event was nerve-wracking on its own.

"But it could have been worse," India told herself as she filled her teacup with hot water in the kitchen before the sun had even risen. She brought the kettle back to its place on the stove and plucked her two slices of toast from the toaster. A portion of eggs was already on her plate. Once she buttered her bread, she was ready to eat. There was grocery shopping and house chores to be done, and she and Rashad had also planned to have dinner at a lovely restaurant. With that added to the list of things to be done, India had little time to lounge around. Her time with Rashad was what she looked forward to most.

As she settled at her now empty table with her breakfast, India used her cell phone as a source of news while eating. She scrolled through headlines with a full mouth until something disturbed her peace.

Three hard knocks on the door startled her badly.

India blinked in complete astonishment before checking the time on her phone. Who could possibly be knocking on her door at six a.m.? Was it one of her neighbors? Once in a blue moon, the elderly woman next door would come over for sugar and other ingredients.

Deciding that this had to be the case, India got up to answer the door. With her hand on the doorknob, she narrowed her eyes. "Who is it?" Just to be sure, she'd ask.

"A special delivery for an even more special girl," came a voice that she'd known her whole life.

India could have cried tears of joy. "Kim!" She flung the door open and greeted her best friend with the fastest, firmest hug she'd ever given anyone.

Kim received her with grace and hugged back. She took two steps inside to balance them both. "Easy there." India sensed her body vibrating as she chuckled. The feeling brought back memories of them laughing on the couch during sleepovers. Oh, how glad she was to see Kim.

Minutes later, they stood in the kitchen over tea. Kim had whipped out her phone to show India photos from her trip. Many pictures had been shared with India via text, but there were still some new ones to view.

"It's all so beautiful. I can almost smell the fresh grass and flowers," India said while admiring a picture showcasing a park in South America. Apparently, Kim and Malik were on break here in Sweetgum for a week following their successful shooting days over there. It was granted to them by the producers of their show, and the cast and crew were given time off too. Everyone would regroup in a new location come this time next week.

Kim swiped to another picture in the same location. This one was of her and Malik. They both wore elegant attire and were standing under a decorated gazebo. India knew what this was. She'd heard about these outfits and the event already. "And as you know, the wedding last Sunday went incredibly well, apart from the absence of our friends and family. But if we knew we'd be getting a surprise week off, we would have done it here." Kim closed her phone and set it down on the counter behind her.

India stroked Kim's arm in a gesture of comfort. "Don't worry. Like we said, you can always use your first anniversary to renew your vows and invite everyone then. If I were you two, I wouldn't have been capable of waiting any longer either. No one is faulting you for tying the knot while you were traveling." She lifted her teacup off the counter. "I'm just glad my best friend is happily married at last."

"I know," Kim held out her hand to show off the wedding band on her finger. "It feels amazing but also different. Different in the best way, of course." She placed her hand on the handle of her cup, which she'd set down. "Different in the best way imaginable."

India laughed with her, sharing Kim's complete elation at this incredible development in her life. "Wow. I can't believe you're here again. I missed you so much it hurt every day. I still can't wrap my mind around you being here." She touched Kim's arm in fascination. "You look amazing while I just woke up." On these words, India touched the red satin bonnet covering her braids. Kim's braids hung loose at her shoulders. They looked impeccable. Only Kim herself could accomplish such a masterful hairdo. India loved the heart she'd braided in cornrows into the side of her scalp.

"No, you're good. You have a glow about you that I noticed through our video chats." Kim sipped her tea then held the cup between her hands. "And I just know that Rashad has everything to do with it."

India's heart soared at the mention of his name. "Yes. I've been a puddle of mush ever since we started dating. I'm glad it looks good on the outside." She giggled with a buzz in her belly. A visiting Kim meant Rashad could finally get to meet her. It just occurred to India now that she should introduce them. "Oh, Rashad and I were going to have dinner this evening. If you'd like to meet him, tonight might be the best chance. Are you and Malik busy?" She used everything in her to contain her own excitement.

"That's an amazing idea," Kim exclaimed, her brows raising, and her eyes sparkling. "We should definitely all meet. No, Malik and I didn't have anything planned, so why not? I'd love to meet the guy who's been getting you out of your comfort zone. I can tell that he's special." She spoke with a teasing air, smiling at India, who giggled in response.

"Yes, he really is," India replied. She imagined Rashad's smiling face from last night. He had handled everything so well. Anyone else might have been turned off, but not him. Could someone be more perfect? She wished they could spend every waking moment together, but that wasn't how life worked. They both had other obligations. She just loved being in his vicinity. No one else had ever made her heart race like him. India had never admitted so out loud, but she could tell that her liking of Rashad had evolved into something else. And boy did she love how it felt. The problem was whether Rashad had experienced the same evolution and if she should tell him. "Anyway, let me catch you up on everything you've missed in town." She temporarily packed up her deep emotions to chat with her bestie.

⁕

"Now that's a show I'd watch," Rashad let Kim and Malik know his exact views on their reality series. Malik had just explained the premise and what they hoped to accomplish.

They'd all introduced themselves to Rashad before settling to eat at the central table of the restaurant. To ensure everyone's comfort and relaxation, Rashad had suggested they have dinner at Mrs. Zhang's Chinese Restaurant instead of the fancy one he'd initially booked. Of course, India had agreed as it was somewhere they all knew and were allowed to speak as freely as they wanted while dining. Luckily, not many came out to eat here tonight, giving them the freedom to be as expressive as they wanted without fear of disturbing.

Malik sat beside Kim across from Rashad and India. He'd put on a simple T-shirt and jeans to eat with them. "Thank you, Sir. We appreciate the support." His flat tone didn't take away from the fact that he seemed genuinely grateful. India could see it in the small smile on his lips.

"So where did you guys say you were headed next?" Rashad left his chopsticks sideways in his empty plate. They'd all eaten to their hearts' content and were waiting for dessert.

"Florida. There are several parks to visit over there that our crew is just dying to film. They keep talking about getting a shot with Malik and an alligator." Kim smiled at her quiet husband.

India saw their server approaching in the corner of her eye. She'd said her name was Aimee and wore a nametag to prove it. Two other waitresses came with her to pick up their plates and empty glasses. They all thanked them for their hard work then continued discussing. "As long as you're careful, you should be fine," she said. "But I do believe you'd hold your own pretty well against one. Not that I'm encouraging violence."

This spurred laughter from the table. Malik's laugh was quite soft in comparison to Kim and Rashad's. India expressed her own joy in a quiet manner too. "This must all be so exciting for you two." She clasped her hands on the now-empty table.

Kim nodded. "Definitely, but while we were off exploring the world, you two were doing the same but within town. You even ventured out of town to compete against Peachwooders in Scrabble matches. I think that you guys just might steal our crown for 'most adventurous couple' if we're not careful."

"I'd say that we're more adventurous when it comes to new ice cream flavors." Rashad faced India. "Have you told her about all of our creations?" He seemed eager to fill Malik and Kim in on what had become a hobby between him and India.

India could never forget to tell Kim about that. "Of course, Kim knows every flavor we've made from scratch. I'm sure Malik does too."

"Yes, he does." Kim put her hand on Malik's on the table. "We've talked about possibly joining you two in putting together a wacky ice cream flavor of our own. But that's only if you two would allow us." She looked at Rashad. "Does the ice cream man approve?"

Judging by Rashad's wide grin and bright eyes, India could infer he was on board.

"Yes, of course!" he said. Rashad went on to explain the ice cream creation process and how sometimes, what flavors that seemed like they may not mesh well could make the best desserts. During his lengthy exposition to an oddly attentive Malik, their waitress returned with the dessert they ordered. India took the time to chime in when she received her vanilla ice cream and chocolate cake. She added onto Rashad's discussion by telling them about a vanilla and almond butter ice cream combo she'd worked on with Rashad some time back. Kim didn't seem too surprised that those flavors complimented each other, but Malik was. He went on to ask questions as to where these innovative ice cream flavors were stored and if he could have some. This was amusing coming from him, but India didn't laugh; she simply told him he could have his own tub once they visited Rashad's parlor where these delicious experiments were stored.

The four enjoyed their dessert then headed out for a short walk down Main Street. Somehow, during their strolling, Malik and Rashad wound up getting ahead of Kim and India. Rashad had asked Malik about his previous job as a park ranger, to which Malik had gone on to give some background. Rashad, being Rashad, had gone on to inquire more and listen quite closely as the reserved man gave more history about himself. He seemed comfortable speaking to India's boyfriend.

India knew Malik's introverted nature as well as Kim did. Seeing him open up with little problems to Rashad brought a smile to her face. He was quite the expert at creating a safe atmosphere for people like Malik and herself to speak without fear. "They're getting along," she said to Kim.

"Yes, they are." Kim's teeth looked even whiter under the street-light they encountered outside the restaurant. It was a quiet night with wafting warm breezes. India liked the ambiance of tranquility better than the lively nights of festivals she'd attended over the past few months. "It's great to see." Kim pouted and placed a palm on her chest. "Rashad is a sweetheart." This whisper showcased just how appreciative Kim was for Rashad. She seemed to be fawning more than providing a compliment.

The proud India giggled her response. "I know. I don't think I've ever met a nicer person." She gazed upon the back of Rashad's head. He and Malik were covering lots of ground. They seemed lost in a world of their own. Last India overheard, Rashad had somehow managed to steer their conversation toward football. If anyone could inform Malik on that, it was him. Rashad's brother was an NFL hotshot. "If I had to describe it," she started, succumbing to the dream-like quality overpowering her view of her boyfriend. "I'd say that spending time with him was like sinking deeper and deeper into a satisfying pool of chocolate. He's not just dreamy but creamy too," she said with a cackle. The analogy might come off as odd, but with her own infatuation currently serving as a snug blanket, no words described him better. She'd often wind up sleeping better due to her own memories of who she'd deemed hers.

"Creamy? That's a first."

India caught herself when Kim snorted. She touched her left cheek while her friend carried on. "Sorry. Sometimes when I think too much about how perfect he is, I lose my sense of reality." She shifted her eyes to the area across the sidewalk. Not a soul trekked its path. Tonight's peace filled her with a certain content. Now and again footsteps and stranded conversations hovered across the atmosphere, but for the most part, they alone served as guests on Main Street. "Every day's a fairy tale with him." When the words left her mouth, Rashad laughed with Malik. The only indication that Malik had done so was his slightly moving shoulders. She wondered what the joke was.

"Sounds like a dream," Kim said, closer than India remembered.

India sensed her friend's breath against her ear and jumped.

Kim leaned away mischievously. "Sorry. I had to, just to pull you out in case you got lost in your fantasies again." She gathered her hands in front of her. "I've heard that if a relationship makes you feel safe, it's special." The pace of her strides slowed down. "Some people argue otherwise, but I definitely agree with feeling safe with your partner." She stroked her wedding band, appearing satisfied. "It's how I was sure Malik would be mine forever. He's amazing."

"I can tell. I was there every step of the way when you two were getting close." India kicked aside a single rock that had popped up in her path. "I definitely believe that what you felt with him is the effect Rashad has on me."

"Oh, really?"

India allowed a vehicle to drive past on the street beside them before answering. "I really do." She brushed her fingertips against her chest. The low neck of her blouse permitted her to feel her own skin. "It's like... I don't just like him. It's more than that. I think I..." Butterflies fluttered their rapid wings across her stomach. India gripped it shortly then knocked the tips of her thumbs together. "No, I know that it's turned into something more. Even after Nevaeh's behavior at the dinner, he's been so sweet. I don't know if that's just a testament to how much I mean to him, but it's beautiful. I just love his spirit." She heard only Rashad's jovial pitch for a second. "Being with him is like celebrating a holiday every day."

Kim seemed moved. "You can say it, you know. I've only seen you two interact over dinner a while ago, but I think I can tell when there's undeniable mutual levels of feelings between two people."

She gave India a short nudge with her elbow. "Tonight might be as good a time as ever to do it."

While the encouragement did motivate India, it also gave her jitters. "You say that like you know exactly what I'm talking about." She squirmed almost unnoticeably, barely twitching her shoulders but sensing tiny insect legs crawling around between her flesh and muscles. She hadn't even admitted it but possibly opening her heart in a deeper sense than agreeing to date Rashad scared her.

"It's not hard to put two and two together," Kim shrugged. "And for the record, I'm really happy for you."

A rush raced from India's heart to her toes. She was somehow both cold and hot all at once. As no words were shared between her and Kim, she found herself pondering in silence. The cracks in the sidewalk were suddenly captivating. Surely now wasn't the best time to say how she felt. Did Kim perhaps mean when she and Malik went on their way? India hadn't intended on inviting Rashad over. Perhaps a more intimate setting outside of spending time with friends might help. "But how do I say that I love him?"

"You say it just like that. Let it roll off your tongue when you tell him." Kim combed three loose braids from her face before moving faster. "We should get going. It's kind of late."

India let Kim stroke her back before catching up to Malik. "Yes. We should." Tonight couldn't be when she told him. India wasn't ready just yet. Just like the time they'd both expressed themselves on her couch, she'd wait until the best possible instance to say those three profound words.

CHAPTER TWENTY

akim had taught Rashad a lot of things growing up. One of them was how to toss a football from one end of a field to the next. It was something Rashad never used but always thanked him for sharing. For a while, he'd believed that every bit of dating advice told to him by his brother would never come in handy either, but after sealing things with India, his brother's wisdom had come in handy.

Every minuscule detail on how to treat a girl like a queen would come flooding back to him when he thought up nice dates. Following their epic dinner with India's friends, he'd wanted to have an amazing time like that with just her. So, after thinking it through at work the next day, he'd dug up Hakim's number for a surprise date idea.

"I can't believe you made everything here," India noted, as she stuck her spoon into her half-eaten scoop of melting strawberry-cherry swirl. She looked absolutely breathtaking with the lake at her back as they sat upon a picnic blanket under the stars. He was lucky she'd been up for this on such short notice. It seemed India was down for anything pertaining to him these days. She'd made it clear that spur-of-the-moment plans ground her gears in the past, but now, things were different.

Rashad just finished putting the last empty food container back in his basket. Sweetgum Lake had never sparkled quite like it did tonight. Perhaps India's radiant grin had something to do with it. "You can't believe I made you ice cream?" He asked as a joke.

She patted him in a chastising manner. "Not just that. I was talking about the dinner, too." The woman scooched up to his side when he put the basket on the grass. "You're not just great with dessert but main courses too. Really. Where have you been all my life?" She placed her head on his shoulder.

Rashad was suddenly in heaven. He fixed himself to make her comfier then looked out at the sparkling lake. "I've been right here in town. You just didn't see me as a viable option for a while."

He sensed air expel from her mouth. "I know. And how stupid I was to think like that." She didn't move her face from his body but slowly looked up.

At this angle, she seemed more innocent than usual. Those big eyes made him putty in her hands. "What is it?" He asked.

India averted her gaze. "Wouldn't it be nice to start a small family?" Her voice was hardly a whisper. "To build a tiny cottage on your dad's farm and raise a boy and girl?" She seemed far from the present moment. "They'd grow up caring for animals. It'd make them empathetic and careful with humans, too. Having a few farm chores will teach them responsibility. They'd be nice kids with big hearts. Or at least I'd want them to be."

Rashad had already envisioned a farm life with India. He hadn't pictured kids, but now he was. The little girl had India's face, and he couldn't think of a more perfect daydream. "They would be if you have a hand in raising them." He kissed her nose.

India squinted under his peck. "But I wouldn't mind just being an aunt. We still have a long way to go, but soon, Nevaeh's going to have a child of her own." She removed her head from his shoulder to look him in the eye. "That'd make me an aunt just like you're an uncle."

He hadn't thought of it that way. "Fun uncle and aunt." Rashad poked his chest with a thumb. "Or do they say 'rich' aunt?"

"Yeah. Rich aunt and uncle," India laughed and touched his cheek teasingly.

Rashad took her hand and held it in his lap. With so many stars twinkling above, it was hard to not feel satisfied. He liked how having so few people around gave the illusion that they'd escaped again. Escaped to another realm where they could sit and speak for hours. "That sounds nice too. When Nevaeh and Preah are busy, we can just babysit and spoil their kids." He stared into the heavens. "Although, I try not to spoil Destiny. Preah hates it when I do."

"As she should. Children need to be told no once in a while but not to things that are good for them." India's eyes sparkled with slyness. "And I personally think that a day to be pampered with an uncle and aunt is good for a kid every now and then. They deserve to be treated well." She held the bottom of her face. "Not that I don't think Nev will pamper her baby. I'm sure she will."

Rashad could picture that happening big time. India had made it clear the kind of girl Nevaeh was. "Having kids to pamper is so fun when you're an adult." He sat back with his hands behind him, keeping him upright as his legs stretched forward. "But I always say to never forget to pamper yourself."

"Yes! I agree." India leaned closer to him. "Which is why I always pictured myself spending more money on a honeymoon as opposed to my wedding." She shook her head. "Having a million people stare at me isn't what I'm looking forward to but kicking back on an island? Yes, please!"

Rashad liked that. "You're so right. Once you get the awkward stuff out of the way, it's time to put everything into enjoying some time off with who you chose to spend the rest of your life with." His heartbeat went off the rails at the idea of having a private island to himself and India. This may never take place, but Rashad liked dreaming. He saw the white sand beach and bending coconut tree as it cast a thick shadow over his and India's bodies. They sat side by side on a recliner seat while holding hands. Seagulls squawked and soaring birds flapped their wings as the tide went in and out.

To bask in the sheer perfection of his position, he shut his eyes with India's body close to his. It may have been a fantasy, but with her skin mere millimeters from his, Rashad had no problem envisioning this perfect sight. Him, her, and the bright, sunny beach.

"I couldn't picture being somewhere gorgeous and remote with anyone else." Her words yanked him from his stupor.

Rashad took a good look at her. She seemed drawn to the view of the lake. He couldn't blame her. It wasn't often that starlight twinkled so radiantly off the surface of clear water. Something about tonight seemed special. It could have been his swirling emotions and rising attraction to India or the breathtaking view, but whatever it was, was magical.

"I have something serious to tell you," India murmured near his cheek.

Rashad's body longed to reconnect with hers as she leaned away from him. He studied her.

She was nervous.

Whatever she had to say, it felt big.

India let out a shaky breath after linking her fingers. She inhaled deeply and mumbled a countdown to herself then looked Rashad dead in the eye. "I know that we've only dated for a short while, but I can't deny how you make me feel."

Rashad sat stunned for all of three seconds. He gradually smiled as India maintained her determined expression. He'd never seen her so earnest. Had she been working up the nerve to say this all night? How precious? "I got the feeling you'd say something like that." He already saw where this was going. "Don't worry, India. I—"

India didn't seem to notice what he was doing. "There's just something about you, Rashad." She laughed on these words with eyes pulsing both relief and fear. "You're understanding, full of care, helpful and patient. I don't know what I did to deserve someone so incredible as a boyfriend, but I'm so grateful for you I can't stand it." She took his hand resting on his lap. "For a while, I'd been pondering on whether my feelings were true or not, but I think I know. It's definitely undeniable." A pure smile stretched across her face and reached her brown eyes. "I *love* you, Rashad. And I think I have for longer than I'd been willing to admit."

He'd let her go on since her small speech seemed to mean a lot to her. Now that all was said and tension had settled, he gave her hand a short squeeze and kissed her knuckle. "India Carr, I'm proud to admit that I've felt the exact same way since I told you I'd developed romantic feelings." He watched the shock wash over her face. "For a moment, I'd feared you'd never reciprocate these deep emotions, but when you started bearing your soul just now, I could tell where things were going." He wanted to leap for joy. "And I'd just like to say that I am extremely happy that I no longer have to hide just how seriously I take loving you." He gently brushed the knuckle of her hand against his lips then planted a tender kiss against them.

"Rashad," she breathed, happiness clear in her voice.

Before he could say her name in response, India tackled him to the ground in an eager hug. It was there as he lay on his back that she planted several kisses across his face. Rashad let her do as she pleased until holding her cheeks and locking eyes with her.

India breathed against his face until grinning widely.

He laughed, and it blew a strand of her freshly-done braids backward. After that, they locked lips in content and pulled their bodies upward to kiss. He wrapped his arms around her, and she did the same to him. They eventually started giggling and instead touched foreheads with eyes closed gently.

"I like being on the same page as you," he said, loving the warmth of her skin.

"Me too." India cupped his cheeks again. She smiled with her eyes while connecting them to his. "For once, I was brave. Last time you bore your soul because I couldn't do it in time. This time, I took one for the team and told you first."

"Yes. And I am so proud of you." He nuzzled her then ended their short embrace. "Just know that I'd never reject you. If I could stay with you forever, I'd like that."

"I feel exactly the same way. Sharing a life together..." India seemed to stop herself from going on.

Rashad wanted her to continue. They'd painted so many pictures this evening. He wouldn't mind painting more. The fact that they both saw futures with each other said plenty. He pictured them being in each other's lives for a while. "Would be fantastic." He went ahead and finished India's sentence.

She simply smiled. "Okay. We should get moving. As much as I'd like to stay out here forever with you, we both have work and obligations." India climbed to her feet and stretched a hand out for Rashad.

He made a show out of dragging himself up with her help, and they both giggled.

Once the two folded their blanket and packed up their meal, he put his arm over her shoulders to walk her off. They commented on the gorgeous ambiance as they traveled. Rashad liked listening to how her eye for detail allowed her to pinpoint what exactly made this spot special. He could honestly listen to her until kingdom come.

They left with their backs to the gorgeous lake where their first 'I love you's were spoken. Rashad believed whole-heartedly that many more would be said as time passed and their devotion grew infinitely.

India was it for him.

The love of his life had been here, in the town he loved, all along. She took her sweet time finding him, to be sure.

But Rashad couldn't imagine a sweeter way to spend the rest of his life than with India by his side.

EPILOGUE

India caught Nevaeh when she nearly fell sideways after opening her car door.

"Be careful," said India, assisting her sister to get out unscathed. Nevaeh seemed shaken from almost toppling sideways. "You're lucky I happened to leave my seat first. I don't know what would have happened if I didn't stop you just now." She smiled tightly at the stares they'd garnered. It was well into the evening, but the glaring streetlights made seeing faces quite simple.

"Thank you." Nevaeh hopped out and closed the door. She had an arm around her belly and bulging eyes. The scare just now seemed to have shaken her. "I've been trying my best to stay off my feet to avoid mishaps, but somehow my clumsiness always catches up to me." She breathed out, then dropped both arms to her side.

India re-adjusted her handbag on her shoulder when Nevaeh locked the car with her key. "Are you sure that you're ready to do this?" She still found it unbelievable that her sister had contacted her for moral support on this big announcement. India was honored to be chosen as Nevaeh's right hand through such an essential event. Sharing such incredible news with close friends and family was much different than letting locals in on the new chapter she'd recently started.

Nevaeh nodded determinedly. "As ready as I'll ever be." She tapped her cheeks. "Now let's go. You're my rock tonight, so don't leave me alone."

India melted when Nevaeh grabbed her arm. "Don't worry. Your friends will be there too. They may not know how important tonight is, but I'm sure they'll catch on." She walked with her sister to the doors of Rochelle's diner. A small whiteboard outside the doors outlined some new recipes Rochelle had added to the menu. "Why didn't you tell them again?"

They walked through the door with Nevaeh's hand on India. "Because I didn't want to risk any of them letting it slip before I could. Plus, it's fun watching them be surprised. I'm sure they'll get a kick out of gasping over my choice to finally let the cat out of the bag tonight." She winked as they left many customers gobbling up their meals.

"I see." India could already hear ecstatic chattering from the far-back table. A collective laugh came from the women sitting in the U-shaped chair around it, and they only grew louder the closer they got. "So it's a different surprise for everyone."

Nevaeh looked eager as they closed in on the table. "Hi everyone."

"Nevaeh!" They chorused elatedly.

India noticed that they'd left a space for her beside Brandi. Coffee cups littered the table, and an empty tray sat at its heart. Everyone seemed more than happy to welcome her sister, each holding a copy of a book India had never read. From an outside perspective, the book club seemed quite welcoming.

"What took you so long? Come sit." Brandi waved at India before gesturing to the space on her left. She and Nevaeh's other friends sat on that side of the table. The older women looked comfortable on the right.

"I will soon." Nevaeh said. All signs of anxiety had long since left.

India could almost see the burning glee behind her bright eyes. Seeing so many people she knew in one place must have given her the courage to announce without fear.

India liked that she'd returned to normal. All seemed right with life once again.

"But first, I have a huge announcement." Nevaeh's teeth were bared in a grin. She looked about ready to explode with anticipation for her own news. Meanwhile, the people she'd spoken to looked on in confusion.

Joanne's eyes narrowed. "Wait. Are you talking about…"

"Shush!" Nevaeh didn't hesitate to silence her. Just a second after doing so, she parted her arms in a silly pose. "I'm pregnant!"

India had expected applause but full-on screams followed the big reveal. She blinked away her surprise while facing the older women. They were the ones who'd shrieked just now. One by one, they slipped from their seats to congratulate her sister. India provided room for them to do so. Nevaeh seemed to have found a family in these people.

All the commotion brought bystanders forward. The handful of customers who'd somehow managed to convince Rochelle to serve them amidst the book club meeting watched in confusion.

India didn't bother explaining anything to them. She was too wrapped up watching her sister receive love and congratulations. The sight was beautiful, to say the least. Rochelle personally planted a sloppy kiss of congrats on Nevaeh's forehead. She left Nevaeh with the instruction to 'give this to the baby,' to which everyone released a chorus of 'aww's.

The entire book club had formed a tight ring around Nevaeh. They'd long since jumped from giving congrats to asking questions. Nevaeh's friends in particular had a lot of them.

"I would have brought kazoos and streamers if I'd known you were doing this today." Courtney had a hand on Nevaeh's back as she spoke above the rising noise. Brandi was on Nevaeh's other side, arm wrapped over her shoulders.

Nevaeh laughed gleefully. "I wanted to surprise you again. I only filled India in on what I was doing, and she was sweet enough to provide moral support." She looked at India with a face that beamed gratitude.

India accepted the kiss Nevaeh blew then shook her head while her sister's friends doted on them. "You would have done it for your sister too. I'm not some kind of icon for showing up." She stepped closer to everyone as they opened their ring. "I'm just glad that everyone in town can finally celebrate with us. I know Nevaeh's been dying to have a baby shower."

Nevaeh gasped. "The sooner the better!" She held her arm up. "Get the word out, Rochelle."

"Why are you looking at me specifically to do that?" Rochelle's twists flipped around as she looked from left to right. The question rightfully prompted laughter from those who knew her garrulous nature. "Okay, fine, I'll let everyone know what's happening."

India couldn't resist giggling.

"Oh. Did you girls hear?" Rochelle said loudly. Her words somehow traveled over the layers of ecstatic outbursts. She wormed her way to the center. "Word on the block says Aliyah will soon be married."

The chatter died down at this announcement. Loud congrats changed to whispers of speculation. Nevaeh picked up the words 'really?' and 'when?' among the muffled sounds. She turned to her sister with an arched brow and found her gasping.

"Aliyah is getting married before Chrysta?" She flicked her right wrist rapidly. "Wait, Chrysta joined our book club." Suddenly, Nevaeh put her hand on her mouth. She seemed frightened while searching her immediate surroundings.

"No, she isn't here today," Brandi assured before placing her palm on Nevaeh's upper back. "This is some interesting news. I always pictured Chrysta to be the one to get married first." Her stance changed, and she now held her hips.

Joanne shook her head profusely with knitted brows. "Aliyah

was always the one who got around more. This doesn't surprise me."

"Got around but never committed." Mrs. Zhang chimed in.

And now, a full-on conversation about the two girls was in motion.

From listening, India could tell that Chrysta had only just started attending book club meetings. The more they spoke, the more she gathered. The family name rang a bell, but she had no details on the sisters. "We'll see." That was all she would say.

India sighed. Life in Sweetgum was far from boring, despite the fact that it was just a small town.

But it was a life she loved.

And she wouldn't have it any other way.

AUTHOR'S NOTE

Thank you so much for reading Forever With You, the sixth book in the Sweetgum Meadows Romance series of stand-alone novels. I really hope you loved it! If you enjoyed this book, please consider leaving it a review so that others may also find it. Also, if you haven't read the first five books, yet, check them out today! Although these are stand-alone novels, the stories all intertwine and progress.

I look forward to introducing you to the other characters in this lovely, family-oriented town where each couple will find their happily ever after.

Would you like to receive bonus scenes and keep up with what's next with my upcoming books? Then, make sure you sign up for my mailing list on my website by visiting ImaniPrice.com.

ALSO BY IMANI PRICE

Book 1: Love Between Us

Book 2: Sweet Sunsets

Book 3: Infinite Kiss

Book 4: Dance With Me

Book 5: In Charge

Book 6: Forever With You

Book 7: Secret Sweethearts

Book 8: Endless Love

Book 9: The Harder We Fall

Book 10: Reservations of the Heart

Book 11: Play by Play

Book 12: Guarded Hearts

Book 13: Healing Hearts

Book 14: Dear Sweetgum

Book 15: Lanterns of the Meadows (novella)

Book 16: Drawn to You

Book 17: Under the Sweetgum Tree

Sweetgum Meadows' Visitor's Guide

To all my lovely readers,

Thank you for reading

www.ingramcontent.com/pod-product-compliance
Lightning Source LLC
Chambersburg PA
CBHW030142010826
48973CB00002B/681